ALSO BY ARTHUR LYONS

THE JACOB ASCH NOVELS
Other People's Money
Fast Fade
Three With a Bullet
At the Hands of Another
Hard Trade
Castles Burning
Dead Ringer
The Killing Floor
All God's Children
The Dead Are Discreet

OTHER NOVELS
Unnatural Causes (with Thomas T. Noguchi)
Physical Evidence (with Thomas T. Noguchi)

NONFICTION
The Blue Sense: Psychic Detectives and Crime
(with Marcello Truzzi)
Satan Wants You: The Cult of Devil Worship in America
The Second Coming: Satanism in America

FALSE PRETENSES

Arthur Lyons

THE MYSTERIOUS PRESS

Published by Warner Books

A Time Warner Company

MYSTERIOUS PRESS EDITION

Copyright © 1994 by Arthur Lyons
All rights reserved.

Cover design and illustration by John Sayles Graphic Design

The Mysterious Press name and logo are registered trademarks of Warncer Books, Inc.

 Mysterious Press books are published by
Warner Books, Inc.
1271 Avenue of the Americas
New York, NY 10020

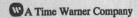 A Time Warner Company

Printed in the United States of America

Originally published in hardcover by The Mysterious Press.
First Printed in Paperback March, 1995

10 9 8 7 6 5 4 3 2 1

For My Partner in Crime,
Gerald Petievich—A Stand-Up Guy,
One of the Few

One

I found the fugitive, John McBride, in a Yum Yum Donuts on Vermont, consuming a glazed twist and coffee with what seemed to be great relish. He did not seem particularly concerned when I informed him that he was the object of an intense LAPD manhunt. All he wanted, he said, was to tell his story to someone from "the outside" before they found him and took him back to Hayvenhurst. Since I was getting paid to listen, I sat down.

McBride was the forty-first conservatorship I'd done for the Superior Court this month. The money sucked—twenty-five dollars per hour—and for the most part, the work did, too, but it beat the hell out of sitting on my ass doing nothing, which was what I'd been doing quite a bit of when a judge I knew called and asked if I'd be interested helping him clear the backlog of petitions clogging his docket. At least that was what I told myself every morning when I dragged myself out to make my daily rounds.

In California, when a person becomes mentally unable to handle his own affairs, a spouse or relative can petition the court to have that person declared incompetent and have him or herself installed as conservator of that person's money.

Before the petition can be granted, however, a state investigator must be dispatched to talk to the person in question, just to make sure he is truly incompetent. So I'd spent the past twenty-eight days in a variety of convalescent homes, auditioning the cast for "Senility on Parade" by asking a list of prescribed questions, such as "Do you know your name?" or "Do you know who the president of the United States is?" If the interviewee did not know the answer to the first or replied "William McKinley" to the second, it was a pretty good indication he or she should not be writing checks.

The seventy-four-year-old McBride didn't look so hot—his sunken-cheeked face had an ashen pallor—but he knew his name, he knew the president's name, and I had no doubt that he knew his wife's name, although he would only refer to her as "The Bitch." He was not surprised to hear that she had petitioned the court to get control of his fortune, which was considerable. In fact, he'd been expecting it. When they had married, McBride had made The Bitch—a flaming redhead forty years younger than McBride—sign a restrictive prenuptial agreement. But his coronary five months ago had shown her a way around it.

After his release from the hospital, McBride's devoted wife had checked him into Hayvenhurst Convalescent Home to "recuperate." Once inside, however, McBride found that all communication with the outside world had been cut off. No mail, no telephone calls. Realizing what was going on, he waited, and when the first opportunity presented itself, he made his break. He'd been on the lam for two hours when I found him.

I used the pay phone outside to tell LAPD to call off their dogs, then got McBride's attorney on the phone and put on the refugee. They talked for some minutes, after which I drove him the three blocks back to Hayvenhurst. We were met by the administrator, a thin, ascetic-faced man named Gingrich, who became quite agitated when I informed him that I intended to recommend a county investigation of his operation and that he'd better make goddamned sure

McBride had access to a telephone but pronto. I gave McBride my card and told him to call if he needed anything, and he thanked me gratefully and assured me he would. Who knew? It could mean a few bucks later when he started to get the goods on The Bitch.

In my car, I checked the appropriate boxes on McBride's conservatorship form, then glanced at the three petitions left. I figured I could knock out two of them and get back to the office before my two o'clock appointment, but the prospect filled me with dread.

Lately, I had begun to see myself in those watery, glaucoma-fogged eyes, in those liver-spotted faces filled with loneliness and despair. I saw myself like them, shuffling aimlessly down corridors going nowhere, sitting on the edge of a bed in a small, bleak room, staring blankly out a window at a bright, sunless day. At the rate I was going, I wouldn't even have a state investigator to talk to. There would be nothing left to petition for. My depression was compounded by the fact that every morning there seemed to be a new pain somewhere, and the old ones were slower to go away. Every morning I discovered some new gray hairs, a new wrinkle, a little more sag under the chin. During the month, I had come face-to-face with my own mortality and I did not care for the countenance.

I stopped at a pay phone and called my service, hoping for a reprieve, something that would require my immediate attention and postpone another trip to Alzheimersville. There were two messages.

The first was that my two o'clock appointment had called to cancel. She had not given a reason and did not say whether she intended to reschedule. Although mildly disappointed, I was not exactly surprised by the news. When she'd called yesterday, she'd sounded tensely hesitant, apprehensive, as if she were not really sure she was doing the right thing. She would only identify herself as "Edith," saying that she wanted to talk to me in person about her "problem" before telling me her last name, and when I'd asked her what exactly was the nature of her "problem," she had been intentionally vague, saying only that it was a "personal matter." From her emotionally keyed-up tone, that translated "domestic case," and I assumed that after having a night to mull it over, she'd simply had second thoughts about hiring a private detective to air her household laundry. I didn't care for domestic cases. They were frequently shrill, acrimonious, and ended with nobody happy—the person you were hired to get the goods on *or* your client. But even a domestic case would have been better than another trip down Memoryless Lane.

The second message was more promising. This one had left a name—Mark Jacobi—and he'd said he had a matter of "extreme urgency" he needed to discuss with me and requested that I call him back as soon as possible. I had no idea who the man was, but I liked the "urgency" part of the message. The more urgent the matter, the less reluctant people were to part with money up front. I dialed the Santa Monica number and a nasally male voice answered on the second ring.

"Mr. Jacobi?"

"Yeah?"

"Jacob Asch."

In the background, I could hear the sounds of street traffic. "Oh. Right. Listen, I gotta see you right away. Where can we meet?"

The accent was midwestern, maybe Chicago. "What's it about, Mr. Jacobi?"

"I want you to tail somebody. Today."

"Who?"

"Before I tell you that, I gotta know if you can do the job. You free or not?"

It only took me a few seconds to make up my mind. The man's pushy tone, which I normally would have found annoying, didn't bother me at all. The man was a life raft on a sea of senility. "It's possible, Mr. Jacobi."

"How about if I come to your office? I can be there in ten minutes."

"You know where it is?"

"The address in the telephone book, right? On Washington?"

"Right." I checked my watch. "Better make it half an hour. It'll take me that long to get there."

He said he'd be there and I hung up, feeling like a condemned man who'd just gotten a last-hour reprieve from the governor. That turned out to be a big mistake on my part, although looking back on it, I can see that there had really been no way for me to know that at the time. There were some things you could not possibly plan for, like looking both ways before stepping off a curb and getting hit by a bucket of cement from fourteen floors up. There was just no way to see it coming.

Two

He was waiting for me in front of my office door, fidgeting impatiently, as I came up the outside stairs. "Mr. Jacobi?"

"That's right. You Asch?"

His handshake was firm, but damp. He was thirty-five or so, of medium height and slender, with pomaded jet-black hair that was slicked back in the fashion that was in vogue again after fifty years. His head was long and thin, and affixed on the sides of it were two very small, lobeless ears that looked like crumpled pieces of paper. His eyes were gray-green, hooded by a heavy epicanthic fold that made them look almost slanted. His teeth were yellowed by cigarette smoke, as were his chewed fingernails. He wore a purple L.A. Lakers windbreaker over a pink Ban-Lon shirt, khaki-colored slacks that could have used a pressing, and brown loafers that could have used a shine.

I unlocked the door and he followed me in. I opened the miniblinds to let in some light, then motioned to two wooden chairs in front of the desk. "Sit down."

He took me up on the offer, crossed his legs, and looked around. I rarely entertained clients at the office. The place was essentially used as a mail drop, message center, and repository for my case files, therefore I'd never bothered to put much money into decorating. The walls needed paint, the carpet needed replacing, and the windows needed washing. Jacobi didn't comment about it, and there was no hint of disapproval as he gave the place the once-over, which was a point in his favor. In fact, there was nothing in his eyes at all that I could read. His face remained impassive as his eyes came to rest on the huge canvas behind the desk, my only prized piece of art.

"A gift from a friend of mine," I said. "The Midnight Skulker from 'B.C.' I'm thinking of using it as a logo on my business cards, although I'm not sure about the copyright problems."

That failed to warrant a smile. He squirmed in his chair, and I asked, "Some coffee, Mr. Jacobi?"

"No, thanks." He glanced at his watch nervously, then licked his lips. "I have to get to work, so I want to get this squared away—"

That was fine with me. "You said you want somebody followed?"

He nodded. "My wife."

Another domestic case. What the hell. It was better than the alternatives. "Why?"

"Every Tuesday, Eileen—that's my wife—goes to visit her mother in Orange County. The old lady is in a nursing home down there. She used to live with us, but our apartment is too small for three people, and it just got to be too much of a strain on us all. So last year, Eileen packed the old lady off to Sunnyvale in Costa Mesa."

My worst nightmare was about to come true—a domestic *and* nursing-home case all rolled into one. "Go on," I said, although I didn't really want him to.

"Two Tuesdays ago, I called Sunnyvale looking for Eileen, and they told me she hadn't been there all day. She got home when she usually did, around six-thirty, and I asked her how her mother was, and she said just fine. When I asked what they'd done, she said that they sat outside and talked, then they allowed her to take her out shopping at the mall."

"Maybe the person you talked to at the nursing home was wrong."

He shook his head. "I called back the next day and talked to a supervisor. Those old people have to be checked out before they can leave the premises. Alice hadn't been anywhere all day."

I didn't say anything and he went on: "Last Tuesday, I called there again. They checked and said Eileen hadn't been there that day, either."

It didn't take any great feat of deductive reasoning to guess why he was here. "Today is Tuesday."

He nodded. "That's why I'm here. I want to know where Eileen goes today." He paused. "What do you charge for something like that?"

"My standard rate is three hundred dollars a day, plus expenses, plus fifty cents a mile."

He hesitated, bit his lip. "Gee, that's kind of steep, isn't it?"

I shrugged. "Those are my rates. I'm sure you can find somebody cheaper—"

"No, no," he said, shaking his head vehemently. "I want you."

"Why?"

He blinked, confused. "Why what?"

"Why do you want me? Did someone recommend me to you?"

He smiled sheepishly. "To tell you the truth, I got your name from the phone book. You were the first in the yellow pages and your address was close by, so I took a shot." He paused and leaned forward intently. "Look, it's important you get right on this. We only live ten minutes from here, but it's ten-thirty already and my wife usually leaves the house by eleven so she can catch the noon Greyhound to Orange County."

"This is all pretty rushed, Mr. Jacobi. Why did you wait until the last minute to hire somebody?"

He tossed up his hands and said in an anguished tone: "I wrestled with my conscience over this thing. I felt as if, well, as if it would be betraying my wife somehow if I hired someone to follow her. I *want* to trust her. But, see, I had a bad experience with my first marriage. My wife was cheating on me. For over a year. Then, one day, I overheard her and her boyfriend joking about it on the telephone, about how stupid I was, that I had no idea about what was going on. I don't want to ever feel like that much of a sucker again. If something is going on, I gotta know now. I can't wait another week. I can't sleep nights."

I smiled and nodded sympathetically, silently demonstrating that I knew exactly what he was going through. "What line of work are you in, Mr. Jacobi?"

"I'm in sales. Ram's Restaurant Supply, over in Culver City." He looked at his watch. "In fact, I gotta get back. I took off work to come over here."

Now came the moment of truth, as they say in the bull-fighting business. "I'll require a retainer of five hundred dollars."

His eyebrows knitted in consternation. "Five? That's two hundred bucks in expenses. All I want you to follow her for is one day. Not even a *whole* day—"

"You'll get itemized receipts for everything," I assured him. "If things run less than that, you will be refunded the difference."

He licked his lips and thought about it. "I didn't think it would be that much. All I got on me is three hundred and fifty bucks. I can give you the rest tomorrow—"

There was something about the man that bothered me, I wasn't sure just what. Whatever it was, however, was not enough to keep me from taking his money. I probably wouldn't see any more than the three fifty, but unless the woman hopped on a plane to Brazil, the chances of my expenses running more than fifty bucks were slight. I didn't care for the nursing-home part, but I tried to look on the bright side. If Jacobi's suspicions were unfounded and his wife did go to visit her mother, I wouldn't actually have to go *inside* the place. "That'll be OK."

He smiled, relieved, and pulled a wallet from his back pocket. He counted out three hundreds, two twenties, and a ten, and handed them across the desk. I put the money into my desk drawer—it looked more professional than just pocketing it—and picked up a pen. "What's your address, Mr. Jacobi?"

"Three-oh-eight Twenty-second Street, apartment 4B, Santa Monica."

I jotted it on a notepad. "Do you have a picture of your wife?"

He shook his head. "No. But I can tell you what she looks like. About five-six, thin, blond hair, about shoulder length. She wears it pinned back. Blue eyes, set kind of wide apart. Oh yeah, and her teeth are kinda bucked. She looks kinda like that actress in those old black-and-white movies, you know, the one with the teeth that stuck out. . . ."

"Gene Tierney?"

"Yeah, that's the one."

"Have any idea what she'll be wearing?"

"Yeah. She was dressed when I left. Powder-blue sweater, black jeans, black leather boots."

"You say the name of the convalescent home in Costa Mesa is Sunnyvale?"

"That's right."

"What's your wife's mother's name?"

"Bufort. Alice Bufort."

There was no real way to ask the question tactfully, so I didn't try. "If she does go somewhere else, if she meets somebody, you want pictures?"

His jaw tightened visibly, the momentary anger faded into sadness, and he shook his head. "No. I just want to know, that's all."

I nodded. "Is the number I called your home number?"

"No. I called from a pay phone. My wife was home and I didn't want to take the chance of her overhearing."

"How will I get in touch with you?"

"I'll get in touch with you tomorrow."

We stood and shook hands.

He smiled strangely. "Thanks for your help, Mr. Asch. This has been eating away at me for a long time. I've wanted to know, and at the same time, I've been afraid to find out. You know what I mean?"

I told him I knew what he meant, and he went out. I listened to his footsteps fade down the stairs, then looked up Ram's Restaurant Supply in Culver City.

The man who answered the phone told me they did have a salesman named Mark Jacobi, but that he was out on a job at the moment. Might somebody else help me? No, thank you, I'll call back.

I opened the desk drawer and transferred the three hundred and fifty to my wallet. It should have felt better there than it did. I should have asked myself why.

Three

At 10:52, I was in position across the street from the address Jacobi had given me. The building was a two-story, L-shaped structure of maybe twenty units that embodied that stamp of blandness characteristic of the fifties. The spirit of the Eisenhower years had even been embodied in the architecture.

The thick shade from the large oaks that lined both sides of the street cooled the morning, and I glanced through the paper while I waited. My mood improved when I came across an article on one of the back pages about Salt Lake City's notorious "panty bandit," who had been burgling women's undergarments from fifteen homes over the past two months. It seemed that the case had taken a surprising turn on Monday, when the bandit mailed his victims' bras and panties back, citing a "religious conversion." One woman, however, a Mrs. Marlita Mapes, told police that instead of her lingerie, she had received twelve dollars in cash and a note saying, "I like these. The $12 should cover it."

I hadn't quite finished the story when a blonde in a powder-blue sweater and black jeans came down the concrete steps of the building and stopped at the curb. She was bony thin, and her complexion was very pale, almost sickly looking. Her eyes were set far apart, and her full lips were permanently parted to accommodate a very prominent overbite. Although the hair color was wrong and she was not nearly as pretty, there was definitely something in Jacobi's Gene Tierney comparison, especially in the shape of the face and the mouth. She adjusted the strap of the black leather bag on her shoulder, then glanced at her watch, then down the street, obviously waiting for something. Two minutes later, a Yellow cab pulled up and she got in.

I waited until the cab turned left at the next cross street, then picked up the tape recorder from the front seat and followed. "Tuesday, December third, eleven-ten. Subject got into Yellow cab, license 765SLW."

The cab headed back down to Wilshire and made a right. At Fifth Street, it turned left and drove a few blocks to the Greyhound station, where she paid off the cabbie and got out. I found a metered space down the street, fed it two dimes, and trotted across to the bus station as a bus was pulling out of the lot. The legend over the front windows said ORANGE COUNTY. Shit. I hadn't seen her get on, but then I'd wasted a few minutes parking. She would have had enough time to board if she already had her ticket. There was one more bus parked in the lot: its destination, Oxnard. I figured I'd better check, just to be sure, and pushed through the front doors of the station.

I stood just inside the doors and did a quick scan of the room. There were a dozen or so people milling around the ticket counter and waiting for buses on benches, but she wasn't one of them. I cursed to myself and was about to make a dash back to the car when she came out of the ladies'room. I walked over to the Space Invaders game in the corner and shoveled in a couple of quarters, keeping my back to her as she took her place in line at the ticket counter. I managed to knock off four alien space ships before she got her ticket and sat down on one of the benches.

The announcement for "Oxnard, Ventura, Santa Barbara"

came over the PA system, and she got up and filed toward the doors to the parking lot with the rest of the people in the room. I walked outside and hung around the corner of the building until she was on board, then ran back across the street. Unless the woman's mother had been moved secretly to another nursing home, it was beginning to look as if there might be something to Jacobi's suspicions.

The bus drove down to Pacific Coast Highway and headed north. The day was pale blue, marked only by a few puffs of cottony cloud, all in all a nice day for a drive. The weekday beach crowd was sparse, but traffic crawled, thanks to a stretch of construction, which the Coast Highway always seemed to be undergoing. I thought it funny that in those brief intervals when the crews had finished whatever it was they were doing, the highway always looked the same.

We drove by the cheap-looking but outrageously priced clapboard houses of Malibu, wedged precariously on the shaky bit of sand between the highway and the sea, past the movie colony, where the houses were considerably more monumental and astronomically priced, and then the traffic thinned and the buildings deferred to scrub-studded hills and the flat calm of the ocean, its blueness mottled only by brown streaks of kelp beyond the silver line of the surf. Even here, however, the death warrants were being tacked up, as every few miles would appear the wooden skeleton of a half-finished condo project or housing tract. Soon, it would all be filled in, from San Diego to Santa Barbara, one continuous strip of apartment buildings and shopping centers made to look like Spanish missions or New England whaling villages. Although I was as ecologically minded as the next man, when that day came, I would vote to allow oil exploration off the coast, just so the bastards would have to look out those big bay windows of their $2 million condos at an army of ugly drilling platforms.

Some miles north, the bus and mine were the only vehicles on the highway. I turned on the radio and ran up and down the dials until I landed on a jazz station that was playing an old Bill Evans tune, "All Blues," when he'd been with Miles and Coltrane and Adderley, the best jazz group that ever was or ever would be, but my mind was humming a different tune, keeping time with every fifty cents on the pavement. We rounded Point Mugu and the road turned inland, past the cyclone fences of the naval station, through a wide agricultural valley of beanfields, and then we hit the outskirts of Oxnard.

Although the Oxnard beachfront boasted some of the most expensive homes on the West Coast, occupied by fugitive moguls and movie stars who had made their way north from the Malibu colony, the downtown area looked like any other California town that has lima bean farming as its central reason for existence. The buildings were dirty brick, the signs in all the windows were either bilingual, or simply in Spanish, to appeal to the trade of the field workers, who made up seven of ten people on the street. This was the kind of town where pawn brokers prospered, where the only art galleries were video stores, where the thick, cloying smell of hot lard and Kentucky Fried Chicken hung over the street like an invisible greasy mist.

I followed the bus into the lot of a modern red-brick bus station with a tall clock tower and watched it disgorge half its load. Mrs. Jacobi was among the departing passengers. She walked over to a Yellow cab, which stood idle at a nearby stand, said something to the driver, and got in.

"Twelve-forty. Subject got into cab, license 451GLU, at Oxnard Greyhound station. Cab is driving west on Pacific."

We drove back toward the ocean down a wide, divided road, and immediately the character of the city began to change. A bridge crossed over a marina filled with the stickmasts of pleasure craft, and the road swept past rows of big, expensive-looking houses fronting the beach. A few years ago, the white sands here had been deserted, but then Rosalind Russell and other celebrities had seen a chance to get away from it all and had built homes. It didn't take long for the developers to follow their lead, and now, beachfront property here was among the highest-priced in the state. The signs on the restaurants were all in English and the sea breezes kept at bay the stink of the fertilizer from the bean-fields inland.

The cab pulled into a wide parking lot and stopped in front of a two-story restaurant called the Whale's Tail. I waited until she had paid off the cabbie and gone inside before I got out of my car.

The restaurant was one of those typical distressed wood, pseudo–Cape Cod clones, decorated in nautical chic, and offering resplendent views of the marina from its huge bay windows. The lunch crowd was sparse and I spotted her immediately, sitting at a window table alone, perusing the menu. The girl at the front desk looked mildly surprised when I asked her for a table away from the windows, but she complied and set me down five tables away from Mrs. Jacobi. I figured the woman's attention would be focused on the view out the windows, and not behind her, and I was right.

She had a couple of glasses of white wine, pausing every so often to look at her watch. I wondered what time Mr. Right was supposed to show. Finally, she ordered lunch, and I was surprised when the busboy removed the other place setting at the table. Maybe he wasn't coming at all. Had she been stood up?

The snapper was on special, so I ordered it, and I matched Mrs. Jacobi's white wines—two more after lunch—with iced teas. I paid my bill with a credit card and waited, nursing a third iced tea. The place was nearly empty at two-thirty, when the waitress went over with her bill. I heard the word "cab," and Mrs. Jacobi thanked her, removed a couple of bills from her wallet, left them on top of the check, and went out. I counted to ten before following.

The cab was on its way out of the lot when I came out of the front doors. I sprinted to my car and we retraced the route back to the Greyhound station. I tailed her into the station, where she sat on one of the wooden benches until three, when the bus was announced for Santa Monica.

I ate bus exhaust for the hour ride back to the Santa Monica station, wondering what her day had been about. Her behavior was curious, but hardly incriminating. Maybe she hadn't been intending to meet anyone at all. Maybe she just needed some time by herself. Lunch, a couple of drinks, a nice view, something to break up the routine of daily housework. There were plenty of places she could have done that closer to home, but maybe she just felt like getting out of town. Somehow, I couldn't make myself buy that one. There had been too much purpose in her movements, as if her day had been precisely planned. And if that was the case, why had she bothered to lie to her husband about going to see her mother?

From the Greyhound station, she caught another cab back home. I hung around outside the apartment building until five, wondering what, if anything, it would mean to Jacobi, then took off, figuring she wouldn't be going anywhere now. Hubby was coming home.

On my way home, I stopped by the office to pick up some billing I intended to catch up on tonight. I pulled into my space and checked my odometer. One hundred and eighteen miles. With the lunch tab, my expenses totaled a little more than seventy-three dollars. The worst Jacobi could stiff me for was twenty-three bucks. And like the man had said, it was only a half-day. The three hundred and fifty was feeling better in my pocket all the time. I trudged up the outside stairs and unlocked the door, and whatever minor feelings of satisfaction I had been feeling were washed away in a good adrenaline start.

Mark Jacobi sat in my chair behind the desk, eyeing me with a ceramic-glazed stare. I didn't have to wonder what his thoughts were of his wife's day. Whatever thoughts he'd ever had were splattered all over the wall behind him.

Four

"You have no idea how he got in here?"

"No."

"Or what he was doing at your desk?"

"No."

His name was Schayes. He was lean, dark haired, in his late thirties, with a large raspberry birthmark on the right side of his jaw that looked as if someone had used his face to clean jelly off a knife. He wore a gray suit with a dark blue tie and a white shirt with little fuzz balls on the collar from being washed too many times. On the lapel of his jacket was a small gold "187" pin—the section number in the California Penal Code for murder.

This was the fourth time he'd taken me through it, asking me the same questions, worded slightly differently each time, to see if I tripped up. The first three times his tone had been hard, his attitude clearly skeptical, but this last run-through, his manner had softened and his style had become friendly, casual, as if he believed me. That made me uneasy, because his gray eyes were not friendly. Like most cops, the man did not seem to have the patience for complexities. When they start to pretend they do, watch out.

He ran his tongue around the inside of his lower lip, making it bulge, and smiled. "He called you up out of the blue, then came over here and hired you to tail his wife."

"That's right."

"Where did he get your name?"

"Out of the yellow pages, he said."

He nodded. "You get many clients drop in that way?" He paused and tried to make the smile look sincere.

"Not many, but some. That's why I pay Ma Bell for the ad."

The coroner's investigator, a slim, attractive, late-twenty-ish brunette, turned to the two ID techs who had been standing around for the past twenty minutes, looking bored while they waited for her to finish up. "OK, I'm done."

They nodded, moved into the room with their evidence kits, and began doing their stuff, collecting, sifting, dusting, while two burly jumpsuited coroner's men bagged the body.

Schayes stepped over to the desk where the coroner's investigator bent down, arranging the tools of her trade in her leather attaché case on the floor. "Any idea when he got it?"

She glanced up at the detective. "From the liver temperature, the room temperature, I'd guess four, five hours. Closer than that, I can't say."

I sighed, relieved. "Well, that lets me out."

Schayes turned back to me, his smile now a frozen smirk. "How do you figure that?"

"I told you where I was all day," I said, shrugging. "I gave you the license numbers of the cabs and showed you the restaurant stub. It'll be easy enough to check out."

"We'll check it out, don't worry," he said, then turned back to the coroner's investigator. "Any ID on him?"

She shook her head. "No."

Schayes' brow bunched. "No wallet?"

She picked up a list and started reading: "Nail clippers, set of keys, a set of lock picks, a white handkerchief, a package of wintergreen Life-Savers, a pack of Marlboros, but no wallet."

"He had a wallet when he was here this morning," I said.

Schayes pierced me with a sharp stare.

"Don't look at me," I said, holding up my palms. "I didn't touch him."

He kept staring.

I stared back. "Maybe whoever killed him took it."

Realizing he was going to get nowhere with that, he turned back to the investigator. "Any doubt about the cause of death?"

She shrugged. "There's no doubt he took a slug, but whether that's what killed him is for the autopsy to determine." She pointed to the round hole in the wall to the left and below the Midnight Skulker, which now resembled a Jackson Pollack. "From where the bullet wound up, as well as the configuration of the blood splatters on the wall, he had to have been shot at a downward angle, from the left. From the powder tattooing around the entrance wound, the muzzle of the gun had to have been in contact with the skin, or close to contact." She made her right hand into a gun, her index finger the barrel, and pointed it down at the left side of Jacobi's head. "I'd say whoever did it stood right about here, put the gun up to the guy's head, and POW!"

The ID tech held up and inspected the cellophane bag containing the slug he'd just taken from the wall. "Looks like a .38." He labeled the bag and put it in his evidence kit.

Schayes asked me: "You own a gun, Asch?"

"A couple."

"What kind?"

"A forty-five auto and a twenty-five auto."

He nodded. "Where are they?"

"At my apartment."

He said nothing, turning toward the sound of a voice behind him. I turned, too, to see Schayes' partner, a detective named Grabner, return after a twenty-minute absence. He was younger than Schayes by six or seven years and built like a halfback, with a smooth, handsome face and close-cropped brown hair. In the short time I'd been exposed to him, he had given the impression that he thought he was a bit of a hotshot. I thought he was a bit of an asshole. He confirmed that for me when he spied the coroner's investigator, who had arrived during his absence, and swaggered over with the demeanor of an actor arriving at a premiere of his latest movie.

Schayes said, "Ms. Bellows, this is my partner, Jerry Grabner. Ms. Bellows is from the coroner's office."

Grabner looked her up and down, a grin of lascivious appreciation on his face. "I guess I'm going to have to spend more time at the morgue."

Schayes asked impatiently, "What did you find out?"

Grabner holstered his dick momentarily and said, "The manager at Ram's says Jacobi left at his regular time, five o'clock."

Schayes glanced sharply at Bellows. "I thought you said a few hours?"

"I said that's what the liver temp indicates," she said, her tone growing defensive.

"Maybe you'd better take it again," Schayes told her curtly.

She met his stare levelly. "There's no need. My reading was accurate."

Schayes manner turned condescending. "Forgive me if I'm wrong, but there would seem to be a need, if this man didn't get here until after five."

Bellows'posture stiffened. "Are you implying, Detective, that I don't know my job?"

"Not at all, *ma'am,*" Schayes said, his tone softer, but because of that, even more condescending. He was getting to her and he liked it. I didn't think it was because he was one of those macho cops who thought women didn't belong in police work; he just liked to get to *everybody.* "But mistakes are made, aren't they? I mean, we are all human beings and to err is human, right? And in light of the facts, we want to be sure, don't we?" Before she could respond, he turned his back on her and said to me: "Well, Asch, looks like you might not be out of the woods yet."

Bellows' lips tightened angrily, but she said nothing. Grabner's eyes were all over her as she bent down and put on her gloves again. "Don't pay any attention to my partner, Ms. Bellows," he told her. "He's just that way. What's your first name, anyway?"

"Ruth."

Bellows pulled open Jacobi's shirt, exposing the incision she had made in the abdomen and unflinchingly inserted the liver thermometer.

Grabner admired her technique and said, "Tell me, Ruth, what's a nice girl like you doing in a job like this?"

She didn't look up, but her voice was now as snide as Schayes'. "It's my calling. Before this, I was an embalmer."

Undaunted, Grabner forged on. "What time do you get off?"

She pulled out the thermometer and held it up to get a reading. "Midnight."

"What say we get together later?"

"I'd love to," she said, offering him a frosty smile. "Go home and eat your service revolver. I'll be right over."

Grabner's expression soured, and Bellows turned to Schayes with a self-satisfied smile. "The same. Happy now?"

Schayes blinked, momentarily confused. "Well, look, with a liver temperature like that, is it possible he could have died just an hour or two ago?"

She turned her back on him and packed up her thermometer. "All I can go by is the charts, Detective. And the charts say four to five hours."

Schayes glowered at her, then turned to the ID tech. "I want a residue analysis on this man's hands."

The tech dabbed my hands with several sticky tabs, then Schayes said, "OK, Asch. Let's go."

I dug my heels into the carpet. There wasn't much to dig into. "Where?"

"To break the news to your client's widow."

Suddenly, conservatorships were starting to look downright enticing. I went out with them, feeling older than ever.

Five

The door was opened by a middle-aged, large-boned man with a heavy face and black curly hair that receded in a widow's peak. He wore a white, long-sleeved shirt, the three top buttons of which were open, exposing a thick mat of black chest hair; black slacks; and black socks, no shoes. Whoever he was, he obviously felt at home here. I wondered if this could be Mrs. Jacobi's secret tryst. Not likely, unless he was dumber than a wooden dime. He would be taking a tremendous chance coming here if he didn't know Jacobi was dead. And if he did know he was dead, he would have to guess the cops would be coming around. His dark eyes blinked questioningly beneath thick black brows. "Yeah?"

Schayes asked, "Is Mrs. Jacobi in?"

The man scanned our faces. "Look, if you guys are peddling some sort of religious message, we're not interested."

Schayes secularized our identities by holding up his ID. "Detective Schayes, LAPD Homicide. This is my partner, Detective Grabner. We'd like to talk to Mrs. Jacobi, if she's in."

The man's face registered surprise. "Homicide? What's this about?"

"It's a police matter," Schayes said.

The man shrugged and pulled open the door for us to enter. The front room of the apartment was a combination living room–dining room with a partition sectioning it off from the kitchen. It was small and furnished without a clue to color coordination or taste. The walls were papered with green plants sprouting tiny pink buds, the carpet was rust, the furniture was overstuffed and covered in knobby fabrics of various clashing hues. The nineteen-inch color TV was on too loud, tuned in to "Wheel of Fortune." The place was filled with the smell of cooked cabbage. The man closed the door behind us and shouted over Vanna White's dumbbell drone: "Eileen!"

The man went over to turn down the television, and Schayes asked him, "Are you a friend of the Jacobis?"

The man gave him a strange look, but before he could answer, a woman emerged from the hallway. She was fortyish, thin, with a narrow head and a small, thin-lipped mouth. Her brown hair was short and coiffed in a mass of tiny ringlets that hugged her head like a helmet. Her brown eyes were receded in their bony sockets, giving the impression she was looking at you from a long ways away. "What is it? Oh, company."

She was singularly unattractive, but when she smiled, something warm spread across her features.

The man turned down the television and said, "These men are from the police."

"Police?" she asked, her smile evaporating. "What happened? Is something wrong?"

I tugged on Schayes' sleeve, but he sloughed me off. "Are you Mrs. Eileen Jacobi?"

"Yes, that's right. What's this about?"

"Your husband, ma'am."

"What about me?" the dark man asked belligerently.

Schayes' gaze jerked toward him. *"You're* Mark Jacobi?"

The man stuck out his sizable chin. "That's right."

I tugged on Schayes' sleeve again, but again, he waved me off irritably as if I were a bothersome fly. "Where do you work, Mr. Jacobi?"

"Ram's Restaurant Supply," the man snapped. "Now what's this all about?"

Schayes pointed at me. "Have you ever seen this man before?"

The man who called himself Jacobi glanced at me, then shook his head. "No. Why?"

Schayes turned to Eileen Jacobi. "How about you, Mrs. Jacobi?"

She looked at me, then shook her head, bewildered. "No."

"And I've never seen her," I broke in.

Schayes' head swiveled toward me. His eyes were steel ball bearings. I shrugged. "I tried to get your attention. This isn't the woman I followed."

"Followed?" Eileen Jacobi asked. "What is everybody talking about?"

"This man is a private detective," Schayes explained. "He claims someone calling himself Mark Jacobi hired him to tail his wife, Eileen, today. From what you're saying, Mr. Jacobi, I take it it wasn't you."

"You take it right," Jacobi growled. "Tail my wife? What, are you guys nuts?"

Schayes tossed me a dirty look. "I'm beginning to think so."

"Do you have a driver's license, Mr. Jacobi?"

Jacobi grumbled but brought out his wallet from his back pocket. He opened it and handed it to Schayes, who glanced at it and handed it back. Jacobi took it resentfully and jammed it back into his pocket, and Schayes said, "Sorry, Mr. Jacobi, but I had to check."

I broke in: "Whoever the man was who hired me, Mr. Jacobi, knew a lot about you. You might know him. About thirty-five, five-ten, thin, kind of greasy black hair, green

eyes that looked almost slanted. Neat dresser. Sound familiar?"

Jacobi shook his head. "I don't know anybody like that."

"How about a woman, thin, blond, eyes set wide apart,
bucktoothed? Maybe she lives in this building?" It struck me
that my voice was beginning to sound a trifle desperate.

"We've lived here for four years," the woman said. "We
know everybody in the building. There's nobody here like
that."

I pressed on while I still had the chance. I had a feeling it
wouldn't be much longer. "Where were you today, Mrs. Jacobi, between the hours of ten and five?"

"At work," she said uncertainly. "I work for AMTRAK."

"What time did you get home?"

"About five-thirty."

"When you got home, did you notice a woman of that description hanging around the building? She would have been
wearing a blue sweater, black jeans, and black boots?"

She shook her head. "I don't remember seeing anyone like
that."

"I don't get it," Mark Jacobi said. "Why would anybody
want to pretend they was me?"

"We don't know, Mr. Jacobi," Schayes said. "That's what
we're trying to find out. We're very sorry to have bothered
both of you. We'll be leaving now."

Schayes glanced at Grabner, who gripped my arm and
started moving me toward the door. Our forward momentum
was stopped by Mark Jacobi, who said, "Wait a sec. You
guys said you're from Homicide. Who got killed?"

Schayes looked at him levelly and said with intentional
vagueness, "That's also what we're trying to find out. Good
night."

In the car, Schayes muttered angrily, "We looked like id-
iots back there." By the way his eyes were boring holes in
me, it was obvious whom he blamed for that.

"Sorry," I said. "But what can I tell you? The guy told me
his name was Mark Jacobi, he worked at Ram's Restaurant

Supply, and gave me that address. The woman he described, right down to the clothes she was wearing, came down that front walkway—"

"You saw her come out of that apartment?"

"No. I only saw her when she hit the street."

Grabner said, "Your story gets screwier all the time, Asch. Why don't you just tell us what really happened?"

I let out a frustrated sigh. "I've *told* you half a dozen times now. Check out what I've given you, you'll find out it's the truth."

Schayes sat in tight-lipped silence for a moment. When he spoke again, his tone was friendly again. "OK. Come on downtown and you can sign a statement. It's more relaxing down there. You can have a cup of coffee, a doughnut. Maybe you'll think of something that'll help us make some sense of the whole thing."

I didn't like the sound of that. "Am I under arrest?"

Schayes smiled and said equivocally, "We hate to use those words. If we use those words, we have to put the cuffs on you. And we don't want to do that if we don't have to, do we, Jer?"

"No," Grabner said, shaking his head sympathetically. "We don't want to do that."

I didn't want them to do that, either, so for a moment, at least, I decided not to push it. I had the feeling that there would be plenty of time for that later. Plenty of time.

Six

They ran me down to Parker Center.

The frequently presented television image of a large metropolitan police station as a swirling, frenzied hive of activity, à la the barely organized chaos of "Hill Street Blues," is just that—a television image. Most LAPD detectives are sent home at five and return only if they get a call to roll on a case. The only detectives on the premises twenty-four hours a day are the homicide boys; evenings, that is a skeleton crew. There was no mad clacking of typewriters, no jangling cacophony of ringing telephones, no prisoners being interrogated or manhandled as we entered the homicide detectives' room on the third floor. Two of the six men in the room had their feet up on their desks and were reading newspapers; one, by his hushed tones and the salacious smile on his face, was engaged in what seemed to be an intimate phone conversation; and three were locked in an animated debate as to where they were going to eat later—Little Joe's or General Lee's in Chinatown. As we passed, one of the trio, an overweight, middle-aged man with a drinker's nose,

28

momentarily suspended gastronomical discussion to inquire, "Whaddya got, Schayes?"

Schayes waved me forward and said, "Guy got his brains blown out in Playa del Rey."

The detective nodded dully. Murder was apparently a less exciting subject to him than chow mein.

Grabner steered me through a pebbled glass door, into a small, stark interrogation room furnished with a Formica-topped table and four wooden chairs. "Siddown."

I sat and Schayes asked politely, "Coffee?"

I looked up at him and smiled. "That's what we came for, isn't it?"

He nodded absently. "What do you want in it?"

"Having experienced the aromatic blend of Homicide coffee before, cream and sugar. Plenty of both."

Schayes nodded to Grabner, who went out to fetch. When he was gone, Schayes sat down and asked in an easygoing tone: "Been in the PI business long, Asch?"

"Fifteen years or so."

"What'd you do before that?"

"I was a reporter."

He nodded and rubbed his birthmark. "I've been a homicide cop eight years myself. I've heard a lot of oddball stories, and I gotta tell you, this one ranks right up there." He said it good-humoredly, as if we were long-time drinking buddies discussing the events of the day over a beer. I hoped he wasn't trying to set me up for a good-guy–bad-guy routine; that one was more than a bit clichéd.

Grabner came back and handed coffee all around. I sipped mine and winced. "As good as I remembered it."

"OK," Schayes said. "Let's go through it once more, just to make sure we have everything right."

My worries about good guy–bad guy were unfounded. They both played bad guys. They took turns hammering away at my story, then took turns making up some of their own.

Why don't you come clean, Asch, and tell us who the stiff

was? There were no signs of forced entry in your office, so how'd he get in? What really happened? You have something on the guy he wanted back? Who was he, some guy you got the goods on whose wife was divorcing him? He blew a fuse and came to your office to kill you? We can buy that, Asch. It was self-defense, right?

An hour and a half later, they seemed to finally get the message that I was not going to break down into a blithering mess and confess, and let up. I could tell they still weren't buying my story, however, so I suggested: "Would it help convince you if I went on the lie box?"

They glanced at each other, and Schayes asked, "You'd be willing to do that?"

"Sure. Why not?"

"Our polygraph guy comes in at seven," Grabner said.

"OK," I said. "I'll be here. In the meantime, I'm tired and I'd like to go home."

Schayes glanced at his watch and said in an amiable tone, "It's after eleven. It seems silly to go all the way back to the beach and come all the way back. We have a nice, comfortable cell here for you to sleep in. That way you'll be fresh, we can wake you up, give you some breakfast, and bring you downstairs first thing. Get it all over with, and if it comes out OK, you can be on your way."

I'd seen this coming from the time they entered my office. Everything since then had been just so much dancing around the maypole. "I'm allergic to jailhouse food."

Grabner smiled. "Oh. You been in jail before?"

"Yeah."

"What for?"

"Contempt of court."

Grabner's forehead wrinkled. "What'd you do, piss off some judge? Hey, I can sympathize with that. Most of 'em are a bunch of whipdicks, anyway."

"How long were you in?" Schayes asked.

"Six months."

Grabner's smile got wider. "You must have *really* pissed

the guy off. What'd you do, tell him to go fuck himself or something?"

"I wrote a story for the *Chronicle,*" I said. "The judge wanted the name of my source. I wouldn't give it to him."

Grabner looked at Schayes with raised eyebrows and said in mock admiration, "Jeez. We got a real stand-up guy here, Phil."

Even though I knew it would be futile, I gave it a shot: "I'll be back at seven. If you want character references, call Jim Gordon in the DA's office, or Lt. Al Herrera at Sheriff's Homicide. They'll vouch for me."

"I'm sure they would," Schayes indulged me. "But it'd be a hell of a lot easier on everybody if you just stayed here tonight."

The line had been drawn and I took a breath and stepped over. At least I'd have the benefit of an attorney. "I want to go home. Now."

Schayes shook his head. "What is it with you? Some kind of compulsion to play hard-ass?"

"I'm not playing hard-ass, Schayes. I'm trying to be cooperative. I've told you everything I know. I've promised I'll be back in the morning. If that's not good enough for you, book me."

He sighed heavily. "You don't leave me much choice, pal. You're under arrest for murder. You have the right to remain silent—"

"Yeah, yeah," I snapped, waving a hand at him in disgust. "Just give me my fucking phone call."

Seven

They gave me a cell by myself. It was a nice cell, as cells go. It had tiered beds, clean sheets, and its own toilet. It was a lot like the cell that had been my home for six months, and although that had been fifteen years ago, the experience was as fresh for me as the acid taste of the coffee I kept burping up every few minutes.

As soon as the door clanged shut behind me, I broke out into the claustrophobic sweats. I paced and told myself it was only for a few hours, that dawn would be coming soon, but every time I looked at the hands on the clock in the hallway they were stuck on the same numbers, so after a while, I forced myself to stop looking. I lay down on the bottom bunk and tried to sleep, but every time I closed my eyes, I felt the walls closing in on me like in some old Republic cliff-hanger serial, and my eyes would snap open, just to check. Of course, the snores, farts, moans, and drunken mumblings from the other cells in the bloc were invaluable aids in helping me stay awake to savor my adventure.

I took up pacing again, trying to get a grip on the fear. When that didn't help, I tried out whatever little I knew of yoga, deep breathing, and self-hypnosis, in an effort to relax. Whether it was my mastery of those oriental disciplines or, more likely, just a crash dive resulting from a total burnout of all my adrenaline reserves, I did manage to finally fall into an exhausted sleep somewhere in the early morning hours.

They woke me at six, and after turning down breakfast, I was taken upstairs to the polygraph room where a sallow-faced operator hooked me up and ran me through a series of questions with monotonic indifference. After my responses were converted into squiggly lines on four different charts, I was installed in another interrogation room and told to wait. To keep myself amused, I began counting the perforated holes in the acoustical ceiling tiles. I was up to 3,406 when the door opened and Schayes and Grabner strolled in casually.

Schayes sat on the edge of the table and dangled his foot, Grabner leaned against the wall and crossed his arms.

"Your lawyer's here raising all sorts of hell," Schayes said sourly. His birthmark looked redder this morning. I hoped it wasn't a gauge of his mood.

"That's what he gets paid to do," I replied with some satisfaction.

Schayes smiled tightly. "You wasted the money. We're dropping the charges."

"Let me guess. I passed the polygraph."

"You passed, all right. You also came out clean on the gunshot residue scan. That doesn't mean much, of course. You could have washed your hands before we got there."

"I didn't."

"It doesn't matter. That's not why we're letting you go."

"Don't tell me it's just because I'm so lovable?"

Grabner said sourly, "We called the restaurant and the cab company in Oxnard. Your story checks out."

"Thanks for doing your job so quickly. It's comforting to know that our police force has competent men like you on the job protecting our well-being."

Grabner leaned forward and glared at me. "You trying to be smart?"

I shook my head. "Not at all. I'm serious. I realize you could have held me for seventy-two hours without charging me."

That seemed to mollify him, and he leaned back. "We do our job."

" 'To Protect and Serve,' " I said, quoting the motto of the LAPD.

"That's right."

We stared at each other for a moment, then I stood up. "I'm free to go?"

"In a minute," Schayes said. "The name William Alan Graves mean anything to you? Aka Billy Ray Graves, aka Billy Ray Allan?"

I gave it some thought. "No. Should it?"

Nonchalantly, he replied, "You knew him by the name of Jacobi."

"You've identified him?"

He nodded. "We were lucky. We got a quick match on his prints. He had a local record."

"Who is—was he?"

He opened a brown manila envelope on the table, pulled out a photograph, which he handed to me. It was a mug shot of Jacobi, front and profile, looking bored posing with numbers. "A small-time burglar, drug dealer, and con man," Schayes said. "A dozen arrests, three convictions."

I handed him back the booking photo. "Any idea who the woman was he had me follow?"

"Not yet."

"Why the hell would he break into my office?"

Schayes shrugged. "Business burglary was one of his specialties. He must have thought you had something in there worth stealing. That's probably why he sent you to Oxnard tailing the broad, to make sure you weren't around."

"But there's nothing there worth stealing. I have no adding machines or computers—"

Schayes rubbed his birthmark. "Only your files. Graves' game wasn't blackmail, at least as far as we know, but he was the kind of a guy who was willing to try his hand at almost anything once. You have any dirt on any rich clients he might have known about and thought he could use for a shakedown?"

I thought about that and came up with zip. "No."

"What kind of cases you been working on lately?"

"Conservatorships for the Superior Court. Nothing that would inspire a B and E, never mind murder."

Schayes thought about that for a moment. "Doesn't sound like it," he agreed. "Maybe something farther back?"

"Not that I can think of."

He slid off the table. "Just in case, go through your files and see if anything is missing."

"What's your theory? That Graves used something from my files to blackmail somebody, called that person up from my office and arranged to meet him or her there, and got blown away for his trouble? It doesn't make any sense."

He shrugged. "Nothing makes much sense at this point."

He had me there. "Is my office still sealed?"

"That's the procedure," Schayes replied.

"How long is it going to stay that way? I do have to make a living."

Grabner grinned at me. "Don't worry. When it hits the papers that you were taken in by a two-bit punk who later got bumped off in your office, you'll have to find another line of work, anyway."

"You know, Grabner, first impressions can be deceiving, but not in your case."

The grin turned into a scowl and he pushed his face at me. "What's that supposed to mean?"

Antagonizing him wasn't going to buy me anything, so I let it slide. "Skip it." I turned to Schayes. "How am I supposed to go through my files if I can't get to them?"

He mulled that one over for a few seconds, then nodded. "I'll see what we can do to expedite things."

They took me downstairs, where Larry Ellman was waiting, briefcase in hand. It was a tearful farewell. "I'm not
going to bother to make any speeches warning you to stay
out of this and let us handle it," Schayes said gruffly. "The
people I talked to about you tell me that would be a waste of
time. To tell you the truth, we've got enough work to do and
I don't mind a helping hand as long as you don't fuck things
up. But if you do come up with something, I want to know
about it, *pronto*. You understand where I'm coming from?"

"Implicitly."

Schayes nodded at Ellman and said through a fake smile,
"Counselor."

They got back on the elevator; the doors slid shut.

"You OK, Jake?" Larry asked, his voice thick with gen-
uine concern. Larry had been my attorney for fifteen years,
and he knew about my emotional problem with jails.

"Yeah, I'm fine, Larry. Thanks for coming."

"The car's outside. I'll drive you home."

"Drive me to my office. That's where my car is." I thought
about it and winced. A taxi ride at a hundred and fifty dollars
an hour. I hoped we didn't hit any traffic.

We got to the front doors and I gratefully drank in the
smog-filtered sunshine, deeply breathed lungfuls of deli-
ciously gray, unsanitized air.

"What in the hell happened?" Larry asked on the way to
the parking lot.

I summarized for him the sequence of events, and he
shook his gray head, bewildered. "Weird. Real fucking
weird. What was this Graves doing in your office?"

"The homicide dicks on the case think he was after something in my files."

"What do *you* think?" he asked as we reached his Mercedes sedan. The alarm bleeped as he disarmed it.

"I don't know what to think at this stage, Larry," I told
him as I opened the door. "But believe me, I intend to find
out."

Eight

The service had two messages, one from a *Times* reporter, the other from a reporter for the Santa Monica *Outlook*. I didn't call either of them back. The less I said, the less they'd have for a story and the less column space the story would be. They might not even run it. I knew the game; I'd played it long enough.

I wolfed down a nuked frozen dinner, luxuriated in a hot shower, shaved, then stretched out on the bed and fell into an exhausted sleep until Bon Jovi blasted me awake two hours later. I dragged myself up, feeling as if I could have slept straight through until midnight, and I might have, but the only thing open at that time was my neighborhood 7-11, and I doubted the Korean cashier there would have the information I wanted. I drove downtown to the Hall of Justice.

The Clerk's Office for the Superior Court had three entries in the index for William Alan Graves: 1987, 1989, and 1990. I filled out request cards for the three cases but was told by the clerk that only the last two files were available today. The 1987 case had been tried in Van Nuys and would have to be ordered. I told her not to bother, that the most recent

37

two would be fine, and she pulled them for me, making sure in her typically officious governmental tone that I would not remove the files from the premises.

The 1989 case was the possession bust. Graves had been driving on Cahuenga in Hollywood one night when he had been pulled over by an LAPD patrol car for an illegal lane change. Noting that Graves appeared to be "under the influence" and observing a half-smoked joint in the dashboard ashtray, the officers conducted a search of the car and turned up an eight-ball of cocaine concealed in the rear wheel well. Graves was found guilty and sentenced to one year in county, of which he served ninety days, plus three years' probation.

He'd still been on probation on 4-8-'90, when he was caught at one-thirty in the morning hauling a load of typewriters and adding machines out of the back door of an office-supply store on Adams. Taking a dim view of Graves' betrayal of the court's trust, the judge slapped the defendant with the nine months left unserved on his dope charge, plus one year for the burglary. Graves was released from county after ten and a half months, and given five years' probation. And round and round it went. If Graves had lived to be seventy, he might have had a 1,400-year probation hanging over his head, but someone had decided to take him out of the system once and for all.

In both cases, Graves had made bail; the first time for five thousand, the second for ten. According to the copies of the bonds in the files, both had been posted by John's EZ Bail Bonds, with an address on Sixth Street. I took down what information I needed, gave the files back to the clerk with obsequious thanks, and left.

John's EZ Bail Bonds was located in a section of dirty brick storefront not far from the county jail. The painted letters on the dirty front window said GET OUT QUICK—24 HOURS—SE HABLA ESPANOL.

The exterior design theme had been carried on through the interior. The walls of the reception room needed washing, the linoleum floor had been blackened by the downtrodden shuffling of the clientele, and the furniture was scarred and dusty. Even the Chicana secretary with the blue eye shadow and rolls of fat hanging over the tight belt of her skirt looked as if her idea of a shower was standing underneath a rain gutter during a storm. She snapped her gum and took my card into the inner sanctum, then came out again and told me to go in.

John, whose last name turned out to be Baines, was a pudgy man with a round, pockmarked face. He wore a long-sleeved, purple shirt, the armpits of which were darkly stained with sweat—in spite of the fact that it was not that warm in the cluttered office—and a wide tie with green and yellow orchids on it. The sparkle of the oversized diamond on his pinkie finger provided an impressive contrast to his dirty fingernails.

He looked at my card, then at me. "What can I do for you, Mr. Asch? You got a client with a problem?"

"Nothing like that, Mr. Baines," I said. "I'm looking for some information about one of your former clients. William Graves. He used you on a couple of beefs back in '87 and '89. Possession and business burglary."

He sat back and regarded me suspiciously. "What kind of information?"

"Anything you can tell me. Last known address, his associates—"

"Associates? I get these assholes out of jail, I don't associate with 'em." He paused, squinting. "What do you want to know about Graves for, anyway?"

I shrugged. "Just trying to make a living."

"Yeah, well, so am I," he said irritatedly. "And I wouldn't be able to, word got out I was passing around information about my clients." He took a business card from the stack on the desk and shoved it at me. "See what it says there? 'Reliable, *Confidential.*' That's why people come to me."

"I appreciate that," I said. "But Graves isn't your client. He never will be again. He got killed last night."

He raised an eyebrow. "Yeah? How?"

"Somebody blew his brains out."

"Who?"

"That's the question."

He frowned. "A question for the cops, not me. What's your interest?"

"Like I said, just trying to make a living." I took out my wallet, extracted two twenties and a ten, and fanned them out on the desk top.

He eyed the bills. "What's that for?"

I shrugged. "I'm making money. No reason you shouldn't."

He thought about it for a good three seconds before deciding. "I don't guess Graves will mind." The money disappeared into his pants pocket, and he hefted himself out of the chair and went to one of the four three-drawer filing cabinets along the wall. He opened the second drawer, rummaged through the files, and pulled out a manila folder. He tossed the file on the desk in front of me and sat back down. "Knock yourself out."

Both bonds were in the file. I concentrated on the burglary case, since it was the most recent. Graves' address was listed as 5566 Hollywood Boulevard, number 22. I ran through the documents and was stopped by a name. "Who is Lexine Woods?"

He held out a pudgy hand. "Lemme see." He looked over the file and said, "Yeah, I remember now. She was the hooker Graves was living with. Graves put up his car for collateral, but she was the one who came up with the grand cash for the bond. I remember, 'cause I was surprised she had that much trick money salted away."

"What did she look like?"

"Skinny. Blond hair. She woulda been pretty if it wasn't for her teeth."

My pulse quickened. "Something was wrong with her teeth?"

"They were trying to get out of her head." He thought for

a moment. "You know who she reminded me of? That old movie actress, what's her name—?"

"Gene Tierney?"

"Yeah, that's her. Gene Tierney."

"You have an address for her?"

He jabbed a finger at the file. "It's right there. The same address as Graves. They lived together."

"You hear from her or Graves since then?"

"Naw. He showed for trial, that's all I cared about."

"She was never a client of yours?"

He shook his head. "Hookers don't need bondsmen. A 647b is a misdemeanor. A hundred-buck fine. They've usually got that on 'em, unless they blew it all on drugs."

I stood up. "Thanks."

"If you talk to Lexine Woods," he said, "you didn't get her name from me."

I smiled. " 'Reliable and confidential' is my motto, too."

Nine

J im Gordon was a short bear of a deputy DA three who had two big passions in his life—Cuban cigars and big-game hunting. His Santa Monica condo looked like the dining room of a hunting lodge, with the heads of kudu, warthog, and Cape buffalo staring from every wall. He also bagged a lot of big game in the courtroom and had sent an impressive number of notorious criminals away for extended stays in Sodomy City. The fact was, Jim hardly ever lost a case, and because of that, he was given some of the toughest cases to win. In spite of his ruthless brilliance in court, however, he was constantly being passed over for promotion, the consensus of the political bureaucracy in the DA's office being that he was "not a team player." Translation: he had told too many of his superiors to fuck off. Which was probably why we got along so well.

I stopped at the first pay phone and called Jim's office. I wanted to make sure I got him before he left for the day. He picked up the phone himself. "Gordon."

"Jim. Jake."

"Jake! I had a call about you last night. A Detective Schayes. Wanted to know if you were the murdering kind."

"What'd you tell him?"

"Only if someone tried to take your rubber duck away. They must have believed me, 'cause when I checked this morning, they said they'd cut you loose."

"Thanks for the concern."

"What was it all about? Who was this Graves character? And what the hell was he doing in your office?"

"I'm trying to find out. That's why I'm calling. I need a favor, for which I am willing to buy lunch tomorrow."

"I don't know about lunch, but what's the favor?"

"I need a rap sheet on a Lexine Woods." I spelled it for him.

"Just a minute." He put me on hold for about three minutes. "Prostitute, huh?"

"So I've been told."

"Looks like you've been told right. Five 647b's. One in '87, two in '88, one in '90, one in '91. She was also arrested for possession of cocaine in '88, but it looks like the charges were dropped on that. Who is she?"

"Graves' live-in girlfriend. I'm pretty sure she was the one he paid me to follow, to get me out of the office. I need packages for her and Graves. Can you pull them for me?"

"Not today."

"Tomorrow?"

"Drop by the office around eleven. If I'm able to get out of here for lunch at all, it'll have to be early. Got a meeting at one. I'll try to have them here then."

"Terrific. One more thing. Graves was on probation. Find out who his probation officer was and if he has a current address for Graves."

"I'll do what I can. It'll depend on what kind of guy he is. Some of those bleeding heart assholes don't like to talk to prosecutors. They see us as The Enemy, trying to put their precious, underprivileged wards in jail. And you know something? They're right."

"You think you got trouble?" I asked him. "I just passed a

Black Angus restaurant. The *g* was burned out on the sign. See you at eleven."

"As long as we don't eat at the Black Angus," he said, and hung up.

The 5500 block of Hollywood Boulevard was east of the freeway, in the middle of glue-sniffing graffiti land. It had a bombed-out, desolate look to it, devastated by the Junkie Blitz. On the littered sidewalks outside dirty brick buildings with bashed-out windows and signs advertising APARTAMENTOS POR RENTA, runny-nosed hypes and quick-eyed thieves surveyed the street and conversed with sick-looking whores. Fifty-five sixty-six was a step up from most of the buildings on the block, but that wasn't saying much. It was a peeling, pink, two-story fleabag motel aptly named the Ratz. A sign outside said that rooms were available by the day, week, or month. They'd forgotten by the hour, which showed that the owner at least had a sense of subtlety. From the number of cars in the parking lot, it looked as if most of the residents worked nights or didn't work at all. None of the models was later than 1980.

I parked next to a blue Nissan pickup with a bashed-in back fender and walked past a fenced-in swimming pool that had no water in it, to number 22. I knocked on the door and waited, and when I got no answer, went down to the manager's office.

The manager, a heavyset, balding man in a loud Hawaiian shirt, informed me through bullet-proof glass that Graves and Woods had moved out eight months ago, no forwarding. The couple had only lived there a few months, and he didn't remember much about them, except that he'd had to break up more than one of their domestic disputes in the middle of the night by threatening to call the cops, and that they'd split owing a week's rent. That was about all I'd really expected to find out, but in this line of work, you had to go through the motions.

On the way home, I picked up copies of the *Times,* the *Chronicle,* and the *Outlook,* and looked through them while I munched on a tuna sandwich at my breakfast table. There was nothing in the broadsheets, but the *Outlook* had it on page two:

MAN SLAIN IN INVESTIGATOR'S OFFICE

The body of William Alan Graves, 32, was discovered in the Venice office of Jacob Asch, a private investigator, late yesterday afternoon, the apparent victim of a homicide. According to LAPD Homicide Detective Ray Schayes, Graves, a convicted felon, broke into the office and was then killed by a single gunshot to the head. The gruesome discovery was reportedly made by Asch, who then telephoned police. Asch was taken into custody, but released this morning. He has not been available for comment. Police have no suspects or motive in the case.

Not too bad. At least Schayes hadn't shot his mouth off about Graves being my client or me being his dupe. I'd have to call him up and thank him. If he and Grabner kept buttoned up about it, in a couple of days the story would be yesterday's news, and I'd be home free. I shook my head. Grabner was probably saving it for the *Times*. Bigger circulation.

I finished my sandwich, then made myself a strong vodka see-through and turned on a forties *film noir* about a woman who believes her husband innocent of murdering a sexy *femme fatale* and talks an alcoholic songwriter into helping her find the real killer. Maybe that was what I needed to solve this case, an alcoholic songwriter. I knew a lot of alcoholics, but I couldn't think of any who'd written any songs. You never knew, though. Maybe one or two of them were frustrated writers and had a tune or two stuck away in a drawer somewhere. Tomorrow, I'd call them all and ask them.

I fell asleep on the couch before the movie was over, so I

never found out if the songwriter uncovered the killer. The telephone jangled me awake at eleven-forty.

"Hello?"

It was Jan O'Connor. "Where have you been?"

I yawned. On the tube, a man was telling me to have my Visa or MasterCard ready so that I could order an "Elvis at the Gates of Graceland Plate commemorating the 1969 Comeback Tour," only $24.95. "Out looking for a hooker."

"Find one?"

"Not the one I wanted."

"Good. I'll be over in ten minutes."

"I'm beat tonight, Jan—"

"I won't stay long. Just a quick drink." I was going to protest, but she said, "Shit. My beeper. Gotta get off. See you in ten."

I hung up, wondering if she had heard about Graves. Probably not. She would have mentioned it if she had. Her professional instincts would have taken over and she would have been wanting to know if there was a story in it, and should she bring a film crew over?

Jan O'Connor was a svelte, thirty-four-year-old, auburn-haired television reporter for KNXT. We had met at a party two months ago and had been dating sporadically ever since. Well, actually, *dating* was the wrong word. It might have been correct in describing the early phase of our relationship, but *coupling* might have been a more apt term for what it had degenerated into of late. Jan approached our relationship like she approached the news—in two-minute sound bites. She would call me up, usually from the freeway on her cellular phone, and if I was up to it, would drop by for a quickie before taking off again, explaining she had to be up early the next morning to cover Assignment Whatever. She would never spend the night, explaining that it was a "thing" she had about sleeping in strange places, which was all right with me. I could take her kinetic hyperactivity for limited periods of time, but anything longer than three hours and I would be climbing the walls. Her conversation, for the most part solil-

quy, consisted almost entirely of some aspect of the news,
either the story she had been on that day (its content, her performance, or what technical problems were encountered
while recording it) or the internal politicking at channel 2
(which anchor had a cocaine or drinking problem, which one
was a bitch, which one had the IQ of a fringe-toed lizard,
etc.), all while she flipped the channels from newscast to
newscast, critiquing the appearance and delivery of the com-
petition. Being long ago purged of all chauvinistic preju-
dices, I didn't resent in the least being used as a sounding
board and sex object, simply because the sex was very good,
if a bit frantic. But lately, she had begun to make odder and
odder requests, the last one having something to do with
handcuffs and a raw egg. Spankings were her big thing, however, and she became incredibly aroused when I took her
over my knee. I got a glimpse of perhaps what fanned the
fires of that passion on our first date, when, over a plate of
tortellini, she leaned toward me with a very intense expression in her eyes and whispered, "I was happy when my
brother died."

I couldn't think of anything to say to that, so I just sat
there, dumbfounded, and nodded.

"I hated him," she went on. "He was Daddy's favorite. He
always got everything. I got nothing."

I made a mental note to check my car for tracking devices.
Somehow, they always seemed to find me. She stared at me
as if expecting some comment, so I did my best. "How did
he die?"

"A motorcycle accident." She paused and lowered her
eyes. "Do you think I'm terrible?"

"Me? No."

Her face flushed, and her breathing seemed to pick up. "I
should be punished. You think I should be spanked for having such bad thoughts?"

"Spanked?" I had to admit, I did find the idea intriguing.

Under the table, she groped my crotch. "Let's get out of
here."

The rest was history.

Eight minutes after the call, there was a knock on the door. I opened it and she said, "Hi," kissed me on the cheek, and came in. She smelled as if she'd been standing over a barbecue. "You smell like smoke," I told her.

"I just did a live remote from a fire. The Standard refinery in El Segundo. You didn't see the story?"

"No."

"It was incredible," she gushed. Her eyes were excited and her cheeks were flushed. "Unbelievable footage."

That was all disasters were to her—footage. The bigger the disaster, the better the footage. The human effects of the event—the cost in lives, the emotional trauma, the agony of loss—all were measured in her world in ten-second sound bites, preferably with tears and a gnashing of teeth. She was one of those strange creatures, impervious to human suffering, who would stick the microphone in the face of a woman whose two-year-old had just been sodomized and murdered, and ask, "Mrs. Wilson, how do you feel right now?"

I viewed such calloused manipulation of people's feelings as representative of everything that was wrong with television news, and we'd gotten into more than one argument about it. In the end, she would dismiss my objections as irrelevant, saying that it was "just the name of the game. Emotions make good footage." Since it was *her* game, and my views were not going to make her change the way she played it, I gave up arguing the point and reconciled our relationship to one of lust. You didn't have to respect a woman to screw her. Sometimes it even got in the way.

She went into the kitchen and poured herself a vodka on the rocks, then sat down on the couch next to me. "Were you really out looking for a hooker?"

"Yep."

She ran a finger teasingly along my ear. "You have something special in mind?"

"Someone, not something. I was looking for a particular

hooker. The live-in girlfriend of the man who got murdered in my office yesterday afternoon."

She sat upright. "What happened?"

I told her what happened and she said sharply, "And you didn't call me? I could have had an exclusive."

"I realize it was thoughtless of me, but when they said I could make one phone call, my attorney's name just popped into my mind, I don't know why."

"You could have called me and *I* could have called your attorney."

"I would have gotten your beeper."

"I would have called back."

"I asked for a suite with a private phone, but they said they were booked and I'd have to settle for a single."

She finally gave up on that track, but the newsroom wheels in her mind were still visibly turning. "Has anybody else picked up on it?"

"Only the *Outlook.*"

"Maybe we can still do something. The guy was only a punk, but the fact that he was blown away in the office of a private eye is a nice hook—"

"Uh-uh."

She grabbed the front of my shirt and stared into my eyes pleadingly. "But, Jake—"

I shook my head. "I'm trying to get less coverage, not more. This isn't the kind of thing that makes good PR."

She crossed her arms, scowled, and pouted with her lower lip. The abused reporter. I pointed at her empty glass. "That *was* a quick drink."

Her pout miraculously vanished, and she flashed a wicked grin. "That wasn't really why I came over."

"No?"

"No." She leaned closer and breathed heavily in my ear. "That fire made me hot."

"Fires are good for that, as man discovered in prehistory."

She poked her tongue inside my ear, sending a chill down to my tailbone. *"Really* hot."

She pulled away and I looked at her. She lifted her skirt above her waist. She had on no underwear. "I was so hot, I took them off on the way over. Gave one truck driver a real thrill."

"I'll bet."

She turned over and lifted her round ass into the air, then looked at me over her shoulder and said in a childlike whimper, "Come on, Daddy, do it to me. I've been a bad girl. Make it hurt."

I made it hurt.

Ten

I woke up at nine, feeling as if I'd been through a chariot race—tied to the back of Ben Hur's. Jan's "quickie" had turned into a marathon and she hadn't left until three. I'd had no idea the creative things one could do with eggs. I was beginning to believe in that "Nature's perfect package" slogan.

The service had five messages for me when I checked in. One was from Schayes, saying that the blockade on my office had been lifted. The other four were from reporters, one television and three newspaper, requesting callbacks. Needless to say, I didn't call any of them back.

After shaving and thoroughly coffeeing myself, I slipped into a pair of gray slacks, a pale-yellow button-down shirt, black loafers, and a gray tweed sports jacket, and drove down to the neighborhood 7-11. The *Outlook* was an evening paper, but the stands had the morning editions of the *Times* and the *Chronicle*. The metro sections of both papers had articles on Graves' shooting, but the forecast was promising. Both articles were brief and scanty in facts, the gist of both being that the shooting death was still a mystery, blah, blah, blah. Both played up the fact that the killing had occurred in my office and that I was still unavailable for comment. The *Chronicle* reporter, James Carnowski, whoever he was, even threw in the tidbit that before I had been a private investigator, I had worked as a reporter for the *Chronicle*. That was just space filler. They'd blown their wad. If I kept ducking them for the next day or so and nothing new surfaced, I would be washed from their minds by whatever new blood was being spilled on the city sidewalks.

At eleven sharp, I walked through the door of Jim Gordon's office, which was cluttered with the usual stacks of legal briefs, trial transcripts, and various books, legal and nonlegal. The place stunk of cigar smoke. Jim was on the phone and not looking happy about it. He waved me into a chair, then tossed a hand in the air. "Yeah? Great. Just fucking terrific. I gotta go into court the day after tomorrow with *that?* Yeah, yeah, I know it's not your fault. Look, just keep the little bastards in custody. *Under wraps. Nobody* talks to them, understand? Not until we get a conviction. Right. 'Bye."

He hung up the phone, picked up the cigar stub from the ashtray on the desk, and jammed it into the corner of his mouth.

"Trouble?" I asked.

"Oh, nothing much. Child molestation case. You heard of Donald Terry?"

I shook my head.

"Nephew of Laurie Dennis."

"The ex–movie star Laurie Dennis? Miss Jesus Freak, Anti-Pornography herself?" Since her retirement, Laurie Dennis had been reborn and had been very vocal in behalf of several national smut-busting organizations dedicated to ridding the kingdom of God—America—of all forms of pornography, hard and soft.

"The same. Her nephew had quite a little kiddie porn operation going. Mail-order tapes and stills. Had a mailing list of four thousand. Ironic, isn't it?"

"Did she know about it?"

He shrugged. "She isn't saying. She had to know he was gay. The guy walks four inches above the floor."

"That alone would be enough to make him an abomination in God's eyes."

"The asshole *is* an abomination, believe me."

"So what was the bad news?"

He peered at me from over the tops of his glasses. "That was the sheriff on the phone. It seems that two of my star kiddie witnesses, former 'actors' in Uncle Donnie's movies —that's what they called him, 'Uncle Donnie'—were arrested last night after they robbed a liquor store and got into a running gun battle with police."

"How old are these kids?"

"Ten and twelve. The twelve-year-old was the wheelman. He had to sit on a stack of telephone books to see over the dashboard. They stole the car, of course."

I had to smile. "Real victim types. They should fill the jury's eyes with tears."

"Tell me about it," he said disgustedly.

"Maybe you can convince them that the trauma of being molested by Uncle Donnie started the poor waifs on the road to crime."

"Are you kidding? Those two thought they were exploiting *him*. No, I just gotta try and keep the other side from hearing about it until the verdict's in. Needless to say, I won't have time for lunch. I have to go over to Juvie and talk to my witnesses." He picked up a brown envelope from his desk and handed it to me. "Your package on Lexine Woods. Couldn't get Graves'. Schayes signed it out and hasn't returned it."

I thought about calling up Schayes and asking if he minded me taking a look at it, but decided to wait. He probably thought he'd already done me a big favor by not feeding me to the dogs, and would make me sit up and beg for another. I opened the envelope and unsheathed its contents while he got back on the phone and made arrangements for his visit to Juvenile Hall.

The woman I had tailed to Oxnard stared at me from the booking photos attached to the top arrest report, Lexine Woods' 1990 beef. So the question of who was finally settled. The question that still remained was why. Maybe Lexine Woods would be able to fill in that blank.

Since the 1990 report was the most recent, I started with it. The home address listed was the Ratz Motel. Of course. The arresting officer, undercover Vice Det. John Kodi, stated that he had been in the bar of the Cameo Room of the Versailles Hotel and had observed the suspect at the bar. Kodi had immediately recognized Woods, because his partner had popped her working another Strip hotel bar the year before. Kodi caught the suspect's eye and she soon approached him. After a few minutes' conversation, she asked him if he wanted to "party." When he played dumb, she fondled his crotch and set a price of a hundred dollars, at which time, Kodi placed her under arrest.

The previous arrests had been made under similar circumstances. All had taken place in hotel bars in the Hollywood—West Hollywood area.

Jim hung up the phone and I asked, "Did you read these?"

"Yeah," he said over his cigar. "The broad should have been arrested for fraud. Impersonating a hundred-dollar hooker. From her picture, she looks like strictly street-bait."

He set his cigar in an ashtray on the desk, then took off his glasses and began cleaning them with a tissue. "It's ironic, but citizen outrage has caused a lot of these gals to become upwardly mobile. West Hollywood complaints are filed in Beverly Hills Municipal Court. Beverly Hills takes a dim view of prostitution, so a couple of years ago, it started handing out five-day mandatory jail sentences instead of the customary hundred-dollar fines. That drove all the West Hollywood whores into Hollywood. The citizens there got all pissed-off about their street being overrun by hustlers, so the court there started doing the same thing. Being more vulnerable to arrest on the street, a lot of the boulevard trash was driven indoors. Now, instead of getting five dollars for a front-seat blow job, they're working hotel bars and getting a hundred a pop from tourists and conventioners."

They furloughed murderers and put whores in jail. Another example of how the system worked for the public good. "Did you find out who Graves' probation officer was?"

He nodded. "Name's Trondheim. An OK guy for a probation officer. He was surprised to hear Graves was dead. The address he gave me is stapled to the back cover of the folder."

It was the Sunset address. Of course. "I'm sure glad these guys keep close tabs on their charges. Graves hasn't lived at this address for eight months."

He put his glasses back on. "I'll call Trondheim and tell him he can pick up Graves for violation of probation."

I stood up. "Thanks. And thanks for the testimonial with Schayes."

"Anytime."

"Good luck with your witnesses."

His expression soured. "Yeah. I can hear them now, the little bastards, wanting to know what I'm gonna do for them if they testify." He thought about it, and said, "I'll offer them a candy bar and hope that's enough. It was enough to get them to drop their pants for Uncle Donnie."

Eleven

The police tape was still across the door and I ripped it off and went in. Evidence of the event was everywhere. Drawers had been left pulled out, two squares of carpet had been cut out and removed behind the desk, as well as a large section of wallboard where the blood had splattered. The Skulker was gone, too, taken away for measurement of drop dynamics and splatter patterns, blood and tissue typing. I would miss him, but they could keep him, unless someone had recently come up with a cleaner for brains that didn't also remove paint.

The desk, filing cabinets, chairs, everything was covered with dusting powder, white on dark surfaces, black on light, where they'd been searching for prints. I wondered if they'd come up with anything. I doubted it. Only sixty percent of violent crimes in this country were solved by arrest, and a vast majority of those arrests were made at the scene of the crime or by a snitch dropping a quarter to his favorite cop. Contrary to what is portrayed on television, most of the other showy stuff—interviewing witnesses, dusting for prints, collecting fibers and hairs—is for the trial, *after* the perpetrator is caught, or for public consumption, to bolster community confidence in the police. Gave the appearance that the police were *doing* something. The tangible and visible residue of their efforts didn't do much to bolster my confidence. It just pissed me off.

I grabbed a bucket from the broom closet down the hall, filled it with water from the bathroom, and spent the next hour exorcising the police presence. Then I phoned Tim Goodman, my contact at Water and Power, and asked him to check the company printout of its customers for William Graves and Lexine Woods. He told me he would get back to me.

While I waited, I started going through my files, trying to find anything that might have been worth a B and E, never mind murder. Nothing jumped off the pages at me. Nothing even twitched.

I put my feet on the desk, sipped coffee, and thought. I took my feet off the desk, stopped sipping coffee and thought. I got up and paced the room and thought. Still nothing. I sat back down at my desk, resumed sipping coffee, and stopped thinking.

Forty minutes later, the phone rang. It was Tim, calling to tell me that neither Graves nor Woods appeared in the company's computers as customers. I thanked him and hung up, then sat there for a while in the dying afternoon light, putting off the inevitable. I could always let the cops handle it.

It *was* their case, after all. I had nothing to do with it, really, except for the fact that the jerkoff had gotten himself whacked in my office. *After* he'd made a chump out of me. For some reason I could not fathom. But Schayes and Grabner would figure it out. I had all the faith in the world in them. They were sterling examples of the intelligence and tenacity of LAPD Homicide. They would doggedly pursue every lead, follow every loose end, until they had put the puzzle together and the killer or killers in jail. Sure they would

So what? What did it matter to me? So the killer was never caught? The *putz* probably got what he deserved.

Anyway, I had no client. Nobody was paying me to play the hunter. But I felt violated. I'd been personally singled out as a patsy, and I wanted to know why. Then, there was section three, paragraph four, of the Private Eye Oath: When a man is killed in your office, you're supposed to do something about it. It doesn't matter what you thought of him. You're supposed to do something about it. You let it slide, you let someone get away with something like that, it's bad for business, bad for detectives all over.

I sighed, mentally preparing myself for the long evening ahead, reluctantly pushed myself out of my chair, and went out.

Twelve

I grabbed a tuna salad at Norm's, then drove down the Sunset Strip to the Versailles.

Hollywood used to be a town of tanned faces and flashing white smiles, beautiful blondes in cashmere sweaters, and high hopes over drugstore soda fountains. Now, the blondes were all bleached, the smiles were rotten from too much speed, and the soda fountains had gone the way of the saber-toothed tiger. The only hopes evident in the faces of the hypes and street hustlers patrolling the sidewalks were for a trick or bail money or a drug connection.

It was too early for much action, so I got a chance to de-brief the bartender while he sliced up limes for the coming rush. His name was Joe, of course, and he'd been working there for four years. He knew Lexine, even remembered the night she'd gotten busted, but said he hadn't seen her lately. Not in the past couple of weeks, anyway.

I worked my way up the Strip, and at ten-thirty, I was sitting at the bar of the Hollywood Roosevelt Cinegrille, half listening to the sounds being laid down by the jazz quintet while I scoped the crowd for Lexine. I didn't spot her, but then my vision was slightly unfocused from the bubbles

59

fizzing in my eyeballs from the eighty-two club sodas I'd imbibed in every hotel bar in West Hollywood and Hollywood. Most of the bartenders I'd talked to—including the one here—denied knowing Lexine, but a couple recognized my description of her teeth. The most recently any of them could place her out and about was four or five months ago.

The soprano sax player went into a solo. He was good, and under other conditions, I would have stuck around to the end of the set, but I'd had it with drinkers and decided to call it a night. I put a five down on the bar and was getting up when a voice to my left said, "I heard you asking about Lexine."

I turned to look at the voice. She was midtwentyish, quite pretty, with a dark complexion and long, straight black hair. Her body looked surprisingly athletic under her clinging white muslin dress. She must have worked out between stints on her back. She had a Perrier in one hand and in the other one of those long, thin brown cigarettes that are fashionable nowadays. She took a deep drag off the cigarette and stared at me coolly. I smiled and asked, "You know Lexine?"

She tapped the end of her cigarette against the ashtray in front of her, and took a sip of Perrier. "Maybe. You a friend of hers?"

"I wouldn't exactly say that. We get together every once in a while, when I get up this way."

She nodded, looked me over. "I'm Sandy."

"Glad to meet you, Sandy. I'm Bill." I took a sip of my soda. "You seen Lexine around?"

"Not in the past couple of nights," she said. "Where you from, Bill?"

"San Diego."

She nodded intently, as if she found that fact incredibly interesting. "In town long?"

"A couple of days. I'm up on business."

She pivoted on her stool to give me all her attention. "What business are you in, Bill?"

"Women's lingerie."

She grinned mischievously. "You're not going to make any money off me. I never wear any."

I pretended to look interested. "No?"

"Want to see?"

"How much?"

Her eyes narrowed suddenly and the smile disappeared. She regarded me with suspicion and turned away. She took a drag off her cigarette and exhaled a cloud of smoke, which hung in the air between us. "How much what?"

I lifted her wrist off the bar and put it on my crotch. "If I was a cop, this would be entrapment. You're safe."

The smile was back. She leaned over and whispered in a tone that was supposed to be seductive: "A girl's got to be careful nowadays."

"Sure," I said.

"What do you have in mind, Bill?"

"You ever do a twosome?"

She ran a long nail gently along my chin. "Ooooo. I like the way you think. But it'll cost you, Bill."

"How much?"

"Two hundred."

"No problem. Where do we find the second half?"

She started to slide off her stool. "I'll make a call."

She stopped sliding when I asked, "What about Lexine?"

"What's with you and Lexine?"

"I have this thing for Gene Tierney."

She stared at me uncomprehendingly.

"Someone I knew a long time ago," I said. "You wouldn't know where I can get in touch with her?"

She shook her head. "She doesn't come around much anymore. Not since she went to work for some outcall service."

"You know the name of the outcall service?"

"Naw." She smiled strangely. "Anyway, you don't want to see Lexine, honey. Not unless you want to go to jail."

"What do you mean?"

"When I saw her two nights ago, she was in the back of a car with two LAPD detectives."

"Where?"

"Outside the International."

If Lexine had been arrested and booked, it should have appeared on her rap sheet. Unless she'd been booked under another name. Of course, she could have been let off with a warning or maybe whoever had picked her up had felt a little horny and wanted a head job before going home. I knew of quite a few of the boys in blue who were not above that sort of thing.

She leaned over and intertwined her arm through mine and said in a breathy voice, "Don't worry, honey, I can dig up somebody a lot better-looking than Lexine."

"You know the detectives?"

She pulled away, her eyes grew suspicious again. "Why?"

I took out a twenty and held it below the bar. Her eyes dropped to it. "I might want to bail her out."

Her eyes narrowed. "What is it with you, anyway? You some kind of fruitcake?"

"Let's just say I'm a dedicated fan."

She continued to stare, so I shrugged and started to pocket the money. It never got there. Her hand deftly intercepted it and plucked it out of my fingers. "One of them. Name's Boetticher."

"Hollywood Division?"

"Yeah."

"Vice?"

"Used to be. But that was a couple of years ago. I don't know about now."

I slid off the stool. "Thanks."

She asked halfheartedly, "What about that twosome?"

"Some other night."

"A fruitcake," she decided, and turned to scan the bar with predatory eyes.

Thirteen

The desk sergeant at LAPD's Hollywood Division informed me in that disinterested, officious tone they must teach at the academy that Detective Boetticher was on the premises but was busy. He took my card without looking at it and told me if I wanted to wait, he'd relay the message that I was here. I thanked him profusely for his courtesy and took a seat.

I shared the bench in the foyer with a young female volunteer for a local drug program, who was waiting to see one of her junkie wards, who had been popped earlier that evening for possession of cocaine and an IV kit, the needle for which she had supplied him earlier in the evening. For twenty minutes, she waxed ecstatic about the success of the program, explaining in a very serious tone that the fact that addicts accepted the free, sterilized needles "proved that IV drug users were willing to go out of their way to protect their health." When I asked her if she'd thought of giving out free memberships to Gold's Gym, she gave me a dirty look and stopped talking.

Ten minutes later, the inner sanctum door buzzed open and a woman stepped out. She was a showstopper, a tall, cool, Scandinavian-looking beauty, dressed in an expensive-looking blue pinstriped suit that had been beautifully tailored to hug all the mesomorphic curves of her body. Her blond hair was pulled back and clasped. She stopped and stared straight at me and I self-consciously looked away. I heard her say something to the desk sergeant and was surprised when she walked over to me and said in a businesslike tone, "I'm Boetticher. You wanted to see me?"

I stood up and clumsily put out my hand. She was slightly taller than my six feet, which would have made her five-eleven or so without her pumps. "Uh, yes, I guess so. My name is Jacob Asch. I'm a private investigator."

She shook firmly and stared at me expressionlessly. "What can I do for you, Mr. Asch?"

She had a narrow face, a straight nose, and a wide mouth, with full lips and very white teeth. Her skin was creamy and flawless. Her eyes were the most unusual color I had ever seen, sort of an icy green flecked with gray. Her gaze was intelligent and appraising. About thirty-two or -three, I guessed.

"I'd like to talk to you about Lexine Woods."

Her smooth brow furrowed. "Who?"

"Lexine Woods. A prostitute. She's involved in a case I'm working on and I'm trying to locate her."

"I suggest you talk to somebody in Vice. I'm Homicide."

The thought of her poking around in my body orifices somehow made the concept of death not altogether unpleasant. "A witness put her with you and another detective in a car two nights ago outside the International Hotel."

Recognition dawned in her eyes. "Ah. That one. So that was her name, Lexine Woods." She waved me forward and said, "Come on into the back. We can talk better back there."

We got buzzed through the door and made a left at the reception desk into a large squadroom filled with desks, only two of which were occupied. "Lucky you caught me here," she said as we walked. "I only came in to type up a report."

She led the way to a desk against the far wall, motioned

me into a chair, and sat down. On top of the desk, behind her name plaque, were two telephones, a stack of arrest reports, and a plastic photo cube. In one of the photographs, Boetticher was receiving some sort of framed award from the chief; in another, she was standing next to the mayor. On the wall behind the desk was a bulletin board on which were tacked various messages. In the middle of the messages, dominating the board were two signs: BITCH POWER and BITCH GODDESS. Next to them was a large faxed cartoon of an old man standing in an alley, his overcoat spread, exposing himself to two surprised passers-by. Beside the old man was a cup and a sign that read SEE WHAT YOUR DICK WILL LOOK LIKE IN FIFTY YEARS—$1.00.

She leaned back, steepled her fingers and asked, "So what kind of a case are you working on and what exactly does Lexine Woods have to do with it?"

"A few days ago, a small-time crook by the name of William Graves was shot to death in my office."

One of her arched eyebrows arched even more. "I thought your name sounded familiar. I read about it in the papers."

I went on: "Graves told me his name was Jacobi and hired me to tail his wife around for a day. He said he wanted to know if she was two-timing him. I followed her up to Oxnard, where she had lunch and sat around for a couple of hours before she caught a bus back to town. I thought it was kind of funny at the time, but in my line of work, you see people do a lot of funny things. It turned not-so-funny when I returned to the office and found Graves there with part of his skull missing."

"So where does this Lexine Woods figure into it?"

"Lexine Woods was the woman I followed. She was Graves' girlfriend, and he obviously used her to get me out of my office. Maybe she knows why."

She unsteepled her fingers and tilted her head back. For the first time, I noticed the white, symmetrically round scar on the right side of her long neck. I had no doubt that its duplicate was on the other side, beneath her brushed blond ducktail. It would be a little bigger, more ragged. Exit wounds usually were. I wondered how she had gotten it.

"I can see why you'd want to ask her some questions," she said, "but I'm afraid I can't help you. I have no idea where you can find her."

"Didn't you arrest her?"

She shook her head. "No."

"But you *did* pick her up—"

She hesitated and stared, trying to decide whether to trust me. After weighing the matter for a few seconds, she said, "About four weeks ago, we rolled on a hooker killing at a motel on the Boulevard. The girl was only nineteen. Hogtied and strangled. From the look of the scene, the freak who did it was into some major S and M, got excited, and crossed over from playtime into reality. The guy had paid for the room with a stolen credit card, but we put together a composite sketch from the motel clerk's description and circulated it among the working girls and spread the word to report any trick they might run into who's into bondage or rough stuff.

"Anyway, a couple of nights ago, my partner got a call from the woman you say is this Lexine, who said she'd just gone on a call at the International that might be the guy we're looking for. We went over there and she got in the car and gave us the story. Apparently, some middle-aged weirdo wanted to tie her up with clothesline and attach clothespins to her body while he masturbated. She got scared and split and called us. The guy didn't match the description of the man we were looking for, but we checked it out anyway and went up to the room. The guy turned out to be the head of a big textile firm in Chicago, out here on a business trip. He about shit when we told him who we were. Started shaking, blubbering, begging us not to call his wife, who was apparently unaware of his extracurricular activities. When we finally managed to convince him that we weren't out to burn him, that we just wanted to ask him some questions, he calmed down enough to tell us he'd been in Europe the week of the murder, showed us his passport to prove it. We threw the fear of God into him and left."

"And you never got an address or phone number for Lexine?"

"Phonies. The name she gave us was phony, too. That's why I didn't recognize it when you mentioned it."

Wonderful. I was beginning to feel like one of the Dead-End Kids. "Her friend said she recently started working for some outcall operation. She mention anything like that to you?"

"No. She said one of the bellboys called her, but she wouldn't give us a name. If the lead had looked good, we'd have pushed her on it, but we figured what the hell. That's a job for Vice, not us."

I sighed. "I guess that's it, then. Thanks for your time."

I stood up and started to leave, but was stopped by a familiar face coming through the door. Lyle Choquette looked about the same as he had six years before, when I'd last seen him—a little softer, maybe, a little grayer. He'd been working Metro Homicide then. We'd met working different angles of the same case and had ended up saving each other a lot of unnecessary legwork by pooling our information.

I greeted him first. "Hello, Lyle."

It took him a couple of seconds, but he finally got it. He smiled and stuck out his hand. "Well, well, if it isn't Jake Asch. What the hell brings you around here?"

"A little business. When did you transfer to this division?"

"Five years ago."

He was in his shirtsleeves, his tie was askew, and as always, liberally freckled with mustard stains. I pointed at them and asked, "Still on the quest for the Grail, I see."

He looked down. "Huh? Oh, yeah. But don't tell my doc. I'm supposed to be laying off the red meat. My cholesterol is up to three twenty."

"You find it yet?"

He grinned. "No, but I'm not giving up."

I had ridden around with Choquette for three days while

we were working that case, and during that time, he had eaten nothing but hamburgers, altering the composition a little each time, onion, no onion, pickle, hoping to relive those halcyon days of youth in which the Burger was King. He was trying to attain, so he said, the Perfect Flashback, one that would last more than a fraction of a second, to experience once more those carefree beach days of no responsibility, of milkshakes and orange pop and the smell of ground beef cooking on an open grill.

Detective Boetticher asked, "You two know each other?"

"Yeah," Lyle said. "From my days at Metro. We wound up working on the same investigation. Asch here is a good PI. One of the best."

She regarded me with renewed interest. Amazing what a good word from a colleague would do. Especially among the closed fraternity of police. "Tell you what I'll do," she said. "I'll ask some guys in Vice about this Lexine Woods. Maybe they'll know something."

"I'd really appreciate it. You have my card."

She nodded. We locked stares. Her penetrating gray-green gaze made me feel off balance, awkward, like a gawky teenager. "By the way, you're the most beautiful homicide detective I've ever seen."

For the first time, she smiled, slightly. There was more amusement in the smile than anything else and it made me feel even more stupid. "Thanks."

She turned and went back to her desk, and I shook hands with Lyle again. He said, "Drop by sometime, we'll shoot the shit. Catch up on old times."

I told him I'd do that and went out, remembering the way Detective Boetticher's lithe form moved elegantly back to her desk. That was my Grail. I'd give two years of my life for a night with that, I decided. The last two years. I'd seen enough in the past month to know they wouldn't do me any good, anyway.

Fourteen

My thoughts were still of Detective Boetticher when I turned the key in the door of my apartment. She projected an aggressive, take-charge attitude that would inspire fantasies in a lot of men who liked their women dressed in scanty Nazi uniforms, complete with jackboots and riding crop. Swastikas and riding crops were not my particular brand of fantasy, but I had always been attracted to strong, competent women. And I did have to admit that I found the image of her dressed in jackboots and nothing else somewhat arousing. Maybe I'd get the chance, who knew?

I turned on the tube on my way through to the living room, turned on CNN, and went into the bedroom. I slipped out of my clothes and pulled on a robe, then came back out to the kitchen, made myself a see-through, and sat down on the couch with the yellow pages. The first entry under the heading "Massage" was "All Blondes." I dialed it.

The breathy receptionist who answered informed me regretfully that they had no girls on staff by the name of Lexine, but that she was sure she could provide a "masseuse" who could accommodate my tastes. I thanked her but declined and quickly hung up. Fifteen minutes later, I'd gotten through the E's—"Escorts Par Excellence"—when there was a knock on the door. I looked at my watch. Twelve-thirty.

I went to the door. "Who is it?"

"Jan."

I opened it and she charged past me into the room. I closed the door and said, "Yes, I'm alone."

She was not listening. She made a beeline for the vodka on the kitchen counter, poured herself a stiff one, and took a hefty swig. She stared past me, her mouth a tight line. "That fucking asshole Jerry."

I assumed that was my cue, so I picked it up. "Jerry who?"

"Weiner."

"Who is Jerry Weiner?"

Her head swiveled toward me and she threw me a withering glance. "My news director. You really don't listen to a thing I say, do you?"

It was hard to deny I tuned her out a good deal of the time. After all, there was just so much chatter about newsroom politics, technical snafus, incompetent cameramen, and catty observations about rival reporters one could absorb without going screaming into the night. Still, I said, "Of course I do."

The fact was, that she didn't listen to anything *I* said, only to her own internal stream of consciousness, which she amplified and broadcast to the world. Radio Free Jan.

"So why is old Jerry an asshole?"

She took a swig of her drink and went back on the air. "He gave my series to Phyllis Kramer."

"What series?"

"'Cannibalism—A Growing Trend or Just a Passing Fad.' The dirty bastard stuck me with 'Satanic Child Abuse.'"

It had to be sweeps week again, that enlightening time of year when the ratings were compiled and network news staffs worked overtime to out-tasteless each other in a desperate effort to rack up Nielsen points. "What's wrong with Satanic child abuse? It's lurid and sensational enough."

She looked at me as if I'd just gotten a fourteen on my SATs. "It's yesterday's news, for god's sake." She waved a hand in the air. "That cannibalism story was my idea, and she ripped it off." She paused and said, "She's fucking him."

"Who is fucking whom?"

"Phyllis. She's fucking Jerry. That's why he gave her the story."

Just to keep up my end of the conversation, I asked, "Which one is Phyllis?"

"You know, I pointed her out last week," she said impatiently. "The redhead, the one who came from Dallas. She's jockeying for the weekend anchor job that's coming open. Barnes is leaving, you know."

I told her I thought I remembered her mentioning it.

"If they give it to her over me, I'll walk. I swear I will. I've had it with those assholes."

The driving motivation that pulled Jan's life along was to become an anchor person before she died. With the passing years, she saw her chances slipping away and it gave her quest an obsessive zeal. She had been passed over twice for the position and was a bit bitter about it, to say the least. I suggested, half-kiddingly, "Why don't *you* fuck Jerry and beat her at her own game?"

For a moment, she seemed to seriously consider the possibility, then shook her head. "I couldn't. The man is a slug. Totally repulsive."

She made herself another drink. I made myself a triple. I had the feeling I was going to need it tonight. I carried my glass back to the couch and sat down.

"If that conniving bitch thinks she's going to move up the ladder by climbing over my back, she's making a big mistake. I'll bury her."

Suddenly, she cut herself off, her attention riveted to the television, where the Asian anchor woman was intoning about a bus crash in Palm Springs that had left seven Girl Scouts dead. The woman finished the story, and Jan shook her head in disgust. "Look at those earrings. They look stupid."

I wondered if the parents of the Girl Scouts on that bus shared her feelings. She blinked and looked at me as if noticing me for the first time. Like a good whiff of ammonia can jolt a dizzy fighter back to reality, the CNN anchor's pendulous earrings seemed to have brought Jan, at least for the moment, out of Newsland and into the temporal world. She pointed to the open telephone book and asked, "What were you doing?"

"Still looking for a hooker."

"Have you found out what happened in your office yet?"

"No, but I'm working on it."

I could see the wheels turning. "If it looks like something significant—"

"I told you, you'll be the first to know." I drained my glass and held it out to her. "How about another drink?"

She came over and took it out of my hand. She made two more and brought them back to the couch. Her mood had changed, the anger had drained from her face, replaced by a coy expression that meant only one thing. She knelt down on the floor in front of me and tugged at the belt of my robe. "Just pretend I'm your hooker," she said as she pulled me into her mouth.

I did as I was told.

Fifteen

I woke up with a case of the post-vodka darts. Things kept darting and skittering away, just out of my line of sight, but when I turned my head to catch the critters, they were gone. I made a pot of coffee and sat at the breakfast table staring straight ahead, ignoring them. After the third cup, the vermin problem was under manageable proportions, and I took out the yellow pages and resumed my telephoning. Four calls later, a female voice answered, "Ladies International."

"I'm a lonely guy from out of town and I'd like some company."

"You've called the right place, sir. Where are you staying?"

"The Hollywood Holiday Inn."

"Is there any particular type of girl you'd prefer?"

"As a matter of fact, there is. I used your service the last time I was in town and I'd like the same girl, if possible. Her name was Lexine."

There was a hesitation. "I'm sorry, sir, but Lexine is unavailable. I can send someone else—"

"No, I want Lexine," I insisted. "When *will* she be available?"

"I'm afraid I can't tell you that, sir. Lexine is out of town. I don't know when she'll be back. But as I said—"

"Thank you," I cut her off, and hung up.

The number was an 818 area code. I got out my address finder and looked up Pacific Bell's current CNA number. CNA service numbers are secret numbers telephone company customer service representatives can call to acquire information necessary to settle customer disputes. Since the telephone company doesn't want the public to have access to the numbers for obvious reasons, they are changed regularly. I paid a connection in the accounting office of Pac Bell to keep theirs current for me.

I dialed the number and a female voice asked, "Ms. Ashton. How may I help you?"

I thickened my voice with a syrupy southern accent and said, "Ashton. That's a lovely name. This is Ed McGrath, with Bell South in Charleston, South Carolina. How you doin' today?"

"Fine."

"That's just wonderful. Ms. Ashton, I have a customer disputing a number on her bill. Says she doesn't recognize the number and can't think of anybody she'd be calling there. Can you give me a name to go with it? Maybe that'll help jog her memory."

"What's the number?"

"818-558-0999."

"Just a moment," she said while she punched it out on her computer terminal. "Executive Automotive Repair."

"How about an address?"

"Four-five-six-six-oh Lankershim Boulevard, North Hollywood."

"Thank you so much, Ms. Ashton. You've been a great help. Have any earthquakes out there lately?"

"Not lately."

"I don't know how you people could live out there. The ground moves under my feet, I'd need a little more information."

She laughed. "We don't have hurricanes."

"You got a point there, you certainly do," I said. "I guess we all got our crosses to bear. Well, thank you very much, Ms. Ashton, and have yourself a great day."

I hung up and thought about it. Executive Automotive Repair. Obviously a front. All that was needed for an outcall operation was a telephone and a person to work it. The customer calls in, places an order—blonde, brunette, or redhead, Caucasian, Black, Oriental, or Hispanic—the receptionist calls whoever is available and dispatches her to the appropriate hotel and room. The front might even be legitimate. Some cars might even actually get fixed there. I got dressed.

North Hollywood was just over the hill from Hollywood and, like her more famous sister, had grown up a child of the movie industry. In the thirties, studios like Warners and Universal and Republic had settled there because of its air and open spaces. Land needed for the sprawling studio lots was cheap and the rocky hills nearby were ideal for shooting B-movie westerns. The glamour, however, ended at the studio gates, and what grew up around the lots was a grid of streets lined with nondescript commercial and industrial buildings. Executive Automotive Repair was on one such street, sandwiched between a retail tile outlet and a Fatburger. It was a newly painted white brick building with double aluminum garage doors open in its front. The sign over the doors, in blue letters, said EXECUTIVE AUTOMOTIVE REPAIR—MERCEDES SPECIALISTS. I parked my Mustang across the street, shoved a quarter in the meter, and jogged across traffic.

The depth of the place made it much larger inside than it appeared from the street. At the back of the room, two mechanics were bent over the open hoods of two Mercedes, both of which were running. The air inside was thick with exhaust fumes. Neither of the mechanics looked up from their work, and I took the opportunity to look around. To my right, on the far end of the room, I spotted a sign that said OFFICE over a window cut into a plywood partition. I went over.

On the unmanned desk on the other side of the window

was an adding machine, a telephone, and a large appointment book. In the room behind the desk, hanging on hooks and in boxes arranged on shelves, were fan belts and other spare parts, and a door leading into another, smaller room. The door was open and through it I could see a very attractive, raven-haired woman seated at another desk, casually filing her nails with an emery board.

"Can I help you?"

I turned to the voice. He was tall and bony, with long dark hair pulled back into a ponytail. The name on his grease-stained overalls was BARRY.

"You the owner?"

He wiped his hands on an orange rag and stared at me expressionlessly. His eyes were deeply set, gray and flat, as if somebody pushed two tarnished dimes into the sockets. "That's right."

"Barry, is it?"

"Yeah."

"My name's Fielding, Barry. I'm with Universal. You were recommended to me as a guy who knows his stuff. I've been having problems with my 560 SL lately, and I was wondering when you could take a look at it?"

"What kind of problems?"

"It's running kind of rough, and lately, it's been stalling out at stoplights," I said. "What do you think it could be?"

He shrugged. "Could be electrical. Or a fuel problem. The car here?"

"No. The wife's got it today. I just wanted to set up an appointment."

He stuffed the greasy rag into his overalls pocket, reached through the window, and pulled out the appointment book. He flipped a page.

"How about Thursday?" I asked.

"What time?"

A telephone rang in the back room, the one on the desk behind the window didn't. The brunette in back picked up and spoke into the receiver, too low for me to make out what she was saying. Out of the corner of my eye, I watched her make notations on a pad.

"What time?" Barry asked again.

"Oh, sorry," I said. "Morning. What time do you open?"

"Eight."

"I'll be here."

"Fielding, you said?"

"John Fielding."

While Barry wrote the name into the box for Thursday, I watched the brunette hang up, then dial another number. She picked up the pad and began reciting what she'd written down to whoever answered at the other end. I turned my attention back to Barry as he looked up and said, "You're down."

"Thanks, Barry. Barry what, by the way?"

"Ayleshire."

I pushed out my hand and smiled broadly. "Good to meet you." Barry's expression remained impassive as he shook my hand limply.

My stomach was growling, so I went next door to the Fatburger and filled it with a double cheese and coffee, then went back across to my car. I fed the meter for the next two hours. A little before one, a black woman driving a red Celica signaled and pulled into the Executive driveway. Ten minutes later, a silver Ford Bronco II headed up the driveway, pausing briefly before pulling out into traffic, heading north. I hunkered down in my seat as she passed me, then realized she had never gotten a look at me—I had been the one doing all the staring. Since she was going my way, I pulled out and followed.

Half a mile away, she pulled up in front of an elementary school, where a line of parents in cars were picking up children under the watchful gaze of an elderly crosswalk guard. I tried to look like a waiting parent and anxiously scanned the faces of the kids on the sidewalks. A tow-headed boy of six or seven separated himself from a small congregation of children and came over to the Bronco. The brunette got out of the car, opened the passenger door for him, and helped him into the high front seat.

She drove into Burbank, made some lefts and rights, and eventually wound up on a residential street lined with blighted elms and rundown stucco homes. She pulled into the driveway of a tiny pink house badly in need of paint and helped the boy out of the car. They were on their way across the sere front lawn to the front door when she noticed me pull up and get out of my car, and stopped. When I was within five feet of her, she stopped me with a slightly defensive tone, "What do you want?"

She was a tall thirty-five, with a lithe body and long dancer's legs. Her features were finely chiseled, with high cheekbones, a long, straight nose, large dark eyes, and a delicately shaped pucker of a mouth. With her long black hair cut across her forehead in bangs, she reminded me vaguely of Veronica from the old Archie comics. I'd always had a soft spot for Veronica.

I handed her a card, which she took hesitantly. "My name is Asch. I'm a private investigator."

She looked up from the card suspiciously. "What do you want with me?"

"I'm looking for someone. I'm hoping you might help me."

That seemed to surprise her. "Me?"

"You work for Ladies International. So does she."

Instantly, both her tone and expression hardened. "What in the hell is this?"

I smiled reassuringly. "If you'll just give me a few minutes, I'll explain. There's no trouble, believe me. In fact, I promise you, it'll be worth your while."

She made no move toward the door. The boy looked up at me, then tugged on his mother's hand. "I'm hungry, Mom."

She frowned, then reluctantly said, "A couple of minutes, that's all."

She unlocked the front door and I followed her inside. The place was very small and slightly shabby, but neat. The blue carpet was worn, the furniture cheap and threadbare. Framed posters of old Bogie movies—*Casablanca, Key Largo, The*

Big Sleep—lined the walls. She said, "I gotta fix the kid something to eat."

She started to put her purse down on a chair, then glanced at me, thought better of it, and took it with her into the kitchen. The boy sat on the floor in front of the TV and turned it on. He changed stations until he landed on a Roadrunner cartoon and proceeded to ignore my presence. I sat on the swaybacked couch and watched Wile E. Coyote get the shit kicked out of him while she opened and closed drawers and cupboard doors in the kitchen. A few minutes later she came out holding a plate with a peanut butter and jelly on white and a glass of milk and handed them to the boy, whose attention never wavered from the screen. She took a chair opposite me, lit up a cigarette, and blew smoke in the air with a bored expression that looked practiced. I'd seen a lot like her, all hardened bluff. She'd taken a lot of blows and wore a mask of contempt to try to make the world believe they hadn't hurt.

I nodded toward the kid on the floor, trying to begin on some ground on which she might not feel threatened. "Cute boy."

Her expression softened momentarily. "Yeah," she said, then her tone soured again. "He's the only thing worth shit that my ex-husband left me."

"How old is he?"

"Eight. You didn't come here to talk about my kid. What's the deal?"

"I work for a personal injury attorney, Ms.—?"

"McNaughton," she said, then added suspiciously? "How did you know where I live, by the way?"

"I followed you from Executive Automotive."

She seemed less than pleased by that, but she'd get over it. She tapped the cigarette into the ashtray in front of her and asked, "So who are you looking for?"

"Lexine Woods."

Her eyes narrowed. "You're the guy who called earlier."

"That's right," I said. "You said she was out of town. You know where?"

She threw me a calculating look. "Why are you looking for her?"

"A year ago, a client of the attorney I work for was involved in a serious automobile accident. It left him paralyzed from the waist down. After several postponements, the case is ready to go to trial. Ms. Woods was a witness to the accident and is important to our case. She promised to testify. But when I went to notify her of the impending trial, I found that the address we had was no longer current. She moved several months back and left no forwarding address. We desperately need to find her. We have her deposition, but that's not nearly as important as her testimony. Of course, she will be handsomely recompensed for her time and trouble."

"How much are you suing for?"

I picked a figure out of the air. "Two million." While she digested that, I poured it on. "You can see how important this is to our client. He will remain in a wheelchair for the rest of his life. His medical bills are staggering. He desperately needs to win this settlement just to live out a life with any semblance of dignity."

She said nothing, but something in her face told me I was getting to her. I glanced at the kid on the floor and decided to appeal once more to her maternal instincts. "He has children, too. Three boys. He'll never be able to play ball with them or do many of the things a father does with his children. As a mother, you must be able to sympathize with his situation."

I was proud of myself. It was a moving scenario, full of human suffering and gut-wrenching pathos. She nodded and looked into my eyes and I knew I had her. "I know what sympathy is," she said. "It appears in the dictionary between *shit* and *syphilis*. How much is it worth to you to find her?"

I took out my wallet and extracted two fifties. I put them on the scarred coffee table in front of her. She stared at the money but didn't pick it up. Her face remained as implacable as her voice. "I have a kid of my own to take care of. I have to think of him."

That was the trouble with the maternal instinct. Once you

activated it, it was hard to control. I took out two more fifties and put them on top of the others.

She took a last drag from her cigarette before grinding it out in the ashtray. She exhaled smoke through her nose and said, "That's pretty chintzy, considering how much money is at stake."

I calculated how many hours of conservatorships I was going to have to put in to make up for the money I'd spent on this investigation so far. "It's as much as I'm prepared to offer."

"Then maybe I'd better talk to your attorney personally."

I picked up the money and said in a hard voice, "Never mind, Ms. McNaughton. I'll find her myself. It might take a day or two longer, but I'll find her."

That gave her pause. She bit her lip and watched the money start to return to the safe haven of my wallet, then said, "OK." She held out her hand and I put the four bills into it. She stuffed the money into her bra and said, "I don't know if she's out of town or not. She hasn't answered her phone or checked in in three days."

Three days. The day Graves called on me at my office. "Do you know where she lives?"

"Shinto Court Apartments in Hollywood."

"Phone number?"

"What do you think, I have it memorized? It's at work."

"You know the apartment number?"

"Ten."

"Thanks," I said, and stood up.

Bugs Bunny was doing a number on Yosemite Sam as I passed the TV. I paused and said to the boy, "Good-bye."

He kept his eyes on the screen. Through a mouthful of peanut butter and jelly, he said sullenly, " 'Bye."

Probably defensive training. Ignore the men Mom brought over, pretend they weren't there. I left quickly, so that he wouldn't have to pretend anymore.

Sixteen

The Shinto Court was on Lexington, an old bungalow court complex fronted by an expanse of balding brown lawn. It looked as if in its heyday in the thirties, it might have been Spanish-style stucco, but at some time in its distant past someone had apparently decided to change its ethnic orientation and had added pagodalike scrollwork to the tile roof, and a wooden purifying gate over the cracked and weedy concrete steps leading into the courtyard. Only in L.A.

In the middle of the courtyard, a red and white mottled carp floated upside-down in a concrete pond. There might have been some live ones in there, but I couldn't penetrate the opaque brown water.

Ten was in the back on the left. Venetian blinds were drawn over the windows. I knocked and waited. I knocked again. Behind the door of the apartment next door, music played softly. Perry Como singing "Wanted." I knew how he felt.

I went back out to the car, unlocked the trunk, and got my set of picks out of the spare tire compartment. When I got back to number 10, Perry Como had been replaced by Ed

Ames. I checked out the deserted courtyard. The blinds were open on several of the windows of the apartments facing Lexine's, but I couldn't see any eyes behind them. I shielded the doorknob with my body and went to work.

The tumblers on the lock were worn and it took less than a minute to crack it. I slipped the tools into my pocket, opened the door an inch, and knocked again, hard. It creaked open and I pretended to be surprised for the benefit of any undetected spectators. I stuck my head through the door and called out weakly, "Hello?"

Nobody answered and I slipped inside and closed the door.

The living room was dismal and dirty, thick with the stale odors of cigarettes and booze. The carpet was a bilious green, the walls were burnt orange, adorned here and there with cheaply framed Toulouse Lautrec prints of the Moulin Rouge. On the chipped Formica coffee table in front of a brown Naugahyde couch were two glasses, a half-empty bottle of Gordon's gin, a triangular ashtray filled with filtered butts, and a small portable charge-account imprint machine. It looked as if Lexine had departed without taking along a primary tool of her trade.

On the couch were a copy of that always-enlightening magazine *People,* and a tabloid whose headline screamed, "Horse Born with Man's Face." Across from the couch against the far wall was an inexpensive entertainment center that held a twenty-seven-inch television, a VCR, and a new-looking stereo. There were no books or shelves to hold them, hardly a surprise. I doubted Graves and his hooker girlfriend read much.

On the counter that divided the living room from the kitchen, next to the telephone and answering machine, was a pad of paper. I went over and checked it out. Blank. Not even any impressions I could run a pencil over, like all smart detectives did in the movies. Feeling cheated, I turned my attention to the rest of the room. It was blank, too.

The light on the answering machine was blinking, and I

rewound the tape and hit the play button. There were half-a-dozen messages for Lexine from Ladies International, telling her to pick up or call in, that she had business to take care of, and one on the day of Graves' demise from a Brad, telling Graves he would meet him "at noon, at the address." I jotted that down on a piece of the pad paper and tucked it into my wallet.

The kitchen was pervaded by the sick smell of rotting meat, the source of which I located in the wastebasket beneath the sink—a box of Kentucky Fried Chicken bones covered with ants. Another trail of ants moved purposefully over the countertop carrying scraps of food from the dirty dishes in the sink.

A plastic raccoon-face magnet held up a calendar on the door of the refrigerator. The dates had been crossed off up to three days ago. I opened the refrigerator and peered inside. There was a frozen Mama Celeste pizza, three cans of Lite beer, some stale bread, butter, a cube of moldy cheese. The cupboards were half-full of mismatched glasses and dishes. I opened the drawers below the counter. Some spotted silverware, cooking utensils, one drawer chock-full of grocery store coupons ripped from magazines. I wondered why she bothered to clip them; from the look of things, they didn't eat home much. I went around the counter, to the bedroom.

The room was small and messy. The bed was unmade, a man's dirty white T-shirt lay over the back of a chair. Also on the chair, staring at me, were a frayed brown teddy bear with its tongue sticking out and a furry, big-eyed replica of Gizmo, that cute little critter from *Gremlins*, before he got wet and started sprouting monsters. They would be Lexine's, of course. Whores all had teddy bears. Nostalgic reminders of innocence lost.

The closet was full of both men's and women's clothes. If Lexine had split she had gone without her wardrobe, not a very likely possibility. On the floor next to a laundry basket full of dirty clothes were two battered suitcases and various pairs of shoes, mostly women's. The black boots she'd had on on the day I'd followed her were not among them. I pawed through the laundry without finding anything that looked familiar.

After going through the pockets of the hanging items and coming up with zilch, I turned my attention to the Mediterranean pressed-wood dresser. She had taken four of the six drawers, but of more interest than what was there was what wasn't—namely, the blue sweater and black jeans she'd worn to Oxnard. I closed up the drawers and went over to the bed.

The drawer of one of the nightstands flanking the bed contained a roll of twenties and tens—maybe two hundred worth—and a checkbook for Lexine Woods at Security Pacific. The balance on the check register showed $356.90. In the other nightstand were a nine-inch battery-powered dildo, a box of Mentor rubbers, a jar of KY jelly, and a key. Graves hadn't taken any chances even with his own girlfriend, not that I could blame him, considering her profession. The key had writing on it, and I picked it up to take a closer look. ULOCKIT 26.

I dropped the key in my jacket pocket and went into the bathroom, turned on the light. The mirror on the cabinet over the sink was flecked with toothpaste, there were long blond hairs in the sink. I opened the cabinet. The usual assortment of stuff was there—razor, shaving cream, face creams, lotions, toothpaste—as well as several brown prescription bottles. One was for Dalmane, another for Dexemil, a third was unmarked. I popped the cap on that one and shook out a palm full of crosstops. A little speed to keep things moving along. I put the bottle back, turned off the light, and went out.

I stepped out into the living room and stopped dead in my tracks. The front door was wide open. The cold hard barrel of a gun touched the side of my head, and a steady voice said, "Police. Put your hands on top of your head."

I followed orders and he said, "OK, turn around, put your hands on the wall."

As I did that, I turned and glanced at my captor. I only managed a brief glimpse of a round moon of a face, a pale dome of a head fringed with dark hair, and a dark mustache before he hooked a foot under my ankle and pulled my leg back. He repeated the procedure with my other foot so that I was resting my weight on the wall, and kept his gun in my back while he frisked me. I could smell his breath. Wintergreen, and beneath that, faint but there, whiskey.

"I can explain, Officer—"

"Shut up," he said, pulling out my wallet. There was silence while he looked through it. Then he said, "PI, huh?"

He resumed frisking me and I prayed to the God of B and E that he would miss the set of picks in my coat pocket. I must not have made the proper sacrifices lately, because he dipped into the pocket and came up with it, along with the locker key.

"My, my. What have we here?"

My eyes rolled up to the ceiling. I was toast.

I heard someone else enter the room, and the cop—if he was a cop—said, "I caught this guy going through the place. His ID says he's a PI. I found these on him."

A familiar voice, one I was hoping to hear again soon, but not quite this soon, said, "This saves us a trip. We were going to have to come see you, anyway, Asch. This is the guy I was telling you about, Art, the one who came around last night."

"Hello, Detective Boetticher."

"Let him up, Art."

The gun eased out of my back and I pushed off the wall and turned around. She was looking very smart today in a blue jacket and skirt over a white silk blouse. The black bag slung over her shoulder was either Louis Vuitton or a good knockoff.

"This is my partner, Detective Carlson."

He was dressed in a rumpled tobacco-colored suit. His brown and yellow striped tie needed pressing, and the collar of his white shirt was frayed. He was shorter than she by an inch or so, older by at least ten years, and more than a bit overweight. He had a fleshy mouth, a wide nose, and large, watery brown eyes that had a strange sadness in them. The 9mm Browning in his hand didn't look sad, though.

"Should I cuff him?" he asked, his voice taut.

She asked me, "How about it, Asch? Should we put on the bracelets, or do you give me your word as a gentleman you'll behave?"

"You have my word."

She said to her partner, "It's OK, Art. I don't think Asch here is going to make any more trouble for himself than he's already in."

Art put the gun away and I casually queried, "Trouble?"

"Burglary is against the law," she said. "Or haven't you heard? Punishable by one to fifteen years."

I shrugged. "Burglary is illegal entry with the intent to commit grand theft or petit larceny. I didn't come here to steal anything. I'm just looking for Lexine Woods."

"What did you expect, she was hiding under the bed or something?"

"The door was ajar. When I knocked on it, it swung open. I called out, but nobody answered, so I came in to investigate."

She pointed to the picks in her partner's hand and her voice acquired an edge, "Right. That's why you needed those."

I said nothing.

Boetticher shook her head disapprovingly. "Possession of burglar's tools is a violation of section 466 of the California Penal Code. Added to illegal entry and burglary, you're racking up some points here."

"You'll never prove illegal entry," I told her, trying to sound confident. "You can get me on the 466 charge, but it's a misdemeanor. Think of all the reports you'd have to fill out. For what?"

Boetticher rubbed her well-formed jawline. "There is

that." She plucked the ULOCKIT key out of her partner's hand and asked, "What's this?"

"Just what it looks like. A storage locker key."

Her gray-green eyes regarded me coolly. "Yours?"

I thought about that. If I said yes and they decided to use the key, I could be buying myself trouble. I felt like a contestant on "Let's Make a Deal with the Law." Choose what's behind door number one and win an all-expenses-paid vacation to Soledad. "No."

"Whose?"

"I don't know. I found it in a drawer by the bed."

Boetticher nodded and smiled, pleased by my response. "What did you intend to do with it?"

"See what's in the locker."

"What do you think might be in the locker?"

"I don't know. That's why I wanted to use the key, to find out."

She pursed her lips. "You know, technically, removing this key from this apartment illegally might be considered burglary. Especially if you intended to steal whatever's in storage."

"Here we go again with this burglary nonsense. I'm not a thief. I only wanted to find out what Graves was into. It might explain what he was doing in my office. Look, I leveled with you about the key. I could have lied, said it was mine—"

"You really going to stick to that 'door ajar' story?"

"Wouldn't you?"

"Why don't you come clean, Asch? What are you doing here, *really?*"

I sighed. "I told you, looking for Lexine Woods."

"How'd you find out where she lived?"

"From an employee at the place she worked. Ladies International. You can check that—"

"Don't worry," she assured me. "We will."

Then it struck me. I'd been so distracted by my own predicament, the significance of them being here had eluded me. If one of the tenants had spotted me entering the apartment and called the cops, uniforms would have rolled on it. If it had been a professional call, it would have been Vice. They were *homicide* detectives. "She's dead, isn't she?"

They both stared at me blankly. "What makes you ask that?"

"Why else would you be here?"

"Maybe she's in jail and we dropped by to pick up her toothbrush," Carlson said. "We *are* devoted public servants."

"When did they find her?"

They glanced at each other and she said, "A city sanitation crew found her early this morning in a dumpster in an alley off Yucca."

"Murdered?"

"The ME doesn't like us to guess about things like that until the autopsy results are in," Carlson said, "but I'd be willing to put a couple of bucks down on it. Of course, suicide's a possibility. She could have gotten into that Hefty trash bag and tied it up, then jumped into the dumpster and strangled herself with a piece of clothesline."

He was a real card. "They fix a time of death yet?"

"No," Boetticher replied. "But at least a couple of days. She was pretty ripe."

"What was she wearing?"

She looked at me hard. "Why?"

"Lexine hasn't checked in with her outcall service for three days. The calendar on the refrigerator is marked off up to three days ago, and the clothes she was wearing when I followed her aren't here. That would indicate she never came home that night, or if she did, she went out again without changing."

She thought about it, then asked, "What was she wearing when you saw her?"

"Blue sweater, black jeans, and black leather boots. Calf length."

She nodded. "That's what she was wearing."

"She must have gotten it right after Graves did. Which would eliminate me as a suspect. I was in jail."

"What makes you think you're a suspect?" Carlson asked.

I shrugged. "Oh, I don't know. I guess I'm just naturally paranoid."

"We'll talk about that later," Boetticher said. "Right now, I want to know what you found when you searched the place."

I didn't like the sound of the "later" part but said, "I've already told you."

"Nothing else? Anything that looked like a trick book, an appointment book, anything like that?"

"No. There are some messages on the machine."

She went over, punched the play button and listened to the messages while her partner made notations in a spiral notebook. "You say you've been to this Ladies International place she worked?"

"Yeah. It's over on Lankershim in North Hollywood. A guy named Barry Ayleshire runs it out of the back of a foreign car garage called Executive Automotive."

She nodded, pointed at the couch. "You sit right over there while we take a look around." She turned to her partner. "Take the bedroom. I'll look around out here."

"How about my wallet?"

"Give it to him, Art."

He handed it to me and I sat on the couch. He disappeared into the bedroom and I could hear the bureau drawers opening and closing. My eyes, however, were on Boetticher's long, muscular legs as she went through the kitchen and repeated my search of the living room. After a while, he came out of the bedroom and said, "Nothing."

Boetticher walked right over to the telephone, reached under the shelf on the counter and pulled out a metropolitan phone book. She thumbed through the yellow pages until she found the one she wanted, ripped it out, and closed the book. She came over to me, pointed a thumb in the air and said, "OK, let's go."

"You really going to take me in?"

She stared at me. "I haven't decided yet. If we don't, it'll only be because Lyle Choquette says you're OK."

"Where are we going?"

"You wanted to see what's in that locker, didn't you?"

They locked up the place and marched me outside to a new gray Dodge so insipidly nondescript that it screamed UNDERCOVER CAR. Carlson drove, I sat in the backseat.

ULOCKIT was on Vermont, in a rundown commercial neighborhood where every other sign was in a language other than English. It was four rows of garage doors facing each other across twin alleys and fronted by a dirty cinderblock wall. The wire gate was unlocked and rolled back from the driveway entrance, and we pulled in and cruised slowly down the alleyway, looking for 26. It was halfway down the alley; Art killed the engine and we piled out of the car. He inserted the key into the padlock and it clicked open and he unhooked it and pulled open the door. The ten-by-ten room was filled with adding machines, computers, check writers, laser printers, typewriters, as well as some VCRs and television sets.

"Looks like your boy was into a little business burglary," Boetticher said to me."

"He'd been pinched for it before."

"Maybe that's what he was doing in your office."

I shook my head. "There's nothing in my office worth stealing and he would have known that. He was there earlier."

Carlson was not paying attention to our conversation. He seemed concerned with more immediate, practical matters. He waved at the storage shed and asked, "What do we do with this stuff? Take it in?"

"We've got better things to do than haul a bunch of adding machines downtown," Boetticher snapped. "Call patrol and have them send a unit. They can take a seized property report and turn it over to Burglary."

"They're not gonna be very happy about it," Carlson remarked diffidently. "We *are* the first officers on the scene. Technically, we're responsible—"

"We're *homicide* detectives," Boetticher reminded him. "There's no homicide involved here. No reason we should do Burglary's paperwork for them."

That closed the matter. Carlson went obediently to the car to call it in. He returned two minutes later and said, "They're on their way."

Liquor fumes floated into the air on his words, and lingered. I wondered where in the car he kept the bottle. Boetticher caught it, too, and frowned at him but said nothing.

Ten minutes later, a black-and-white pulled into the driveway, and two young patrolmen got out. "What do we have?" one of them asked.

Their sour expressions confirmed Carlson's prognosis when Boetticher filled them in, but they didn't say anything about it. When we got back into the car, Boetticher said, "Let's pay a visit to Ladies International. You don't mind a little side trip, do you, Asch?"

I didn't mind. Every hour out of jail was an hour well spent to me.

Seventeen

Ayleshire's head jerked up from beneath the hood of the Mercedes he was working on, like an animal at a water hole that had just sniffed the scent of danger. He sauntered over, wiping his hands on a rag and warily watching Boetticher and Carlson look the place over in that way only cops or mob guys thinking of taking over a place do. He recognized me and frowned, then tried weakly, "Your appointment isn't until Thursday, Mr. Fielding—"

Carlson held up his badge. I noticed his hand shook a bit. "Detective Carlson. This is Detective Boetticher. You the owner?"

Ayleshire raked his bottom lip with his teeth. "Yeah, that's right. Name's Ayleshire." He turned to me and asked contemptuously, "You're a cop?"

"Never mind about him," Carlson said. "We're here about one of your employees, Mr. Ayleshire. A Lexine Woods?"

Ayleshire looked Carlson straight in the eyes and said, "I don't have an employee by that name."

Boetticher gave him a cold stare of her own. "You're not going to try to get cute with us, are you, Mr. Ayleshire?"

"What do you mean by that?" he asked, his gaze swiveling toward her.

She took in a breath. "Lexine Woods'body was found this morning. She was the apparent victim of a murder."

He blanched at the news. "Murder?"

"That's right."

He recovered his composure, said, "I don't know anything about any murder. And I don't know any Lexine Woods."

Ignoring the protest, Boetticher said, "We want to see your trick book. We want the names, addresses, and credit card numbers of everyone she saw for the past two months. And we want them now."

Determined to ride out the bluff, Ayleshire adopted a hostile tone: "I don't know what the hell you're talking about. This is a garage. I fix cars. Or didn't you read the sign outside?"

She stepped forward and looked down on him, her voice slow and even, as if trying to hammer a lesson into the mind of a child with a learning disability: "You should be turned in to the Better Business Bureau for false advertising, Ayleshire. This is a whorehouse. And you are a pimp. Not that I care. We're not interested in your operation, although I'm sure Vice would be, if you want us to let them know."

Ayleshire's face reddened. "You have a warrant?"

"A warrant," Boetticher repeated. She stopped and turned to Carlson. "We have a warrant, Art?"

Carlson patted himself down as if searching for one.

"Geez, I guess in my haste, I forgot to bring one. You want me to go back and get one?"

She nodded. "That's only fair. Mr. Ayleshire would like to see one before he shows us around." She turned back to Ayleshire. "That's what you want, isn't it, Mr. Ayleshire?"

Ayleshire nodded defiantly, his courage up now. "That's right."

"Fine. While my partner is downtown trying to find a judge to issue one, I'm going to lock all your doors and handcuff you to one of your cars just to make sure you don't try to illegally take anything off the premises, and we can all sit down and wait for him to come back, which may take eight or nine hours. *Then* we'll see your book. And after that, I'll call up Vice and the IRS so they can make sure you've declared all the income you've made from the back room there." She pulled out her cuffs and turned to Carlson. "Go ahead, Art—"

"Wait, wait, wait," Ayleshire said, throwing up his arms in surrender. "If I give you what you want, you gonna leave me alone?"

"I told you, we have no interest in your operation, only murder."

It didn't take him long to figure out he didn't have any choice. "This way."

The black woman I'd seen driving in earlier looked up as we walked in and immediately hung up the phone. She didn't know who we were, but she knew *what* we were and her eyes rolled up to the ceiling as she took an unpleasant trip down memory lane. "Sheeit."

"It's OK, Inez," Ayleshire assured her. "These officers just want to take a look at the records. There's no heat."

Her features relaxed, but then hardened into contemptuous defiance as she stared at us. Ayleshire opened the top drawer of the three-drawer filing cabinet and pulled out a small, plastic-bound appointment book. He handed it to Carlson, who flipped it open and began leafing through the pages. He nodded and closed the book. "This is Lexine's. You keep separate books for all your girls?"

"You said you just wanted Lexine's—

"Just answer the question," Carlson answered gruffly.

"Yeah."

Carlson dropped it into his pocket, and Boetticher asked, "Lexine complain about any of her customers getting rough with her? Anything out of the ordinary recently?"

Ayleshire shook his head. "Not to me. But I don't talk to the girls much."

She turned to the black woman. "How about to you?"

"She didn't say nothin' to me."

Boetticher looked back down at Ayleshire. "She do any business on the side?"

"How would I know?"

Boetticher nodded and said to Carlson, "Let's go."

Ayleshire took a step forward. "What about the book?"

"It may be evidence in a murder investigation," Carlson said. "If not, we'll get it back to you."

When we got outside, I asked, "So what now?"

Boetticher smiled. "Well, I'll tell you, Asch, you've been cooperative. I think we'll let you slide this time." She turned to Carlson. "What do you think, Art?"

"I think I need a drink."

"I could use one myself," I said, feeling immensely relieved.

"Code Three, Art," Boetticher said.

Eighteen

The Code Three was a cop's bar on Cahuenga, with dark wood paneling and flashing red lights behind the bar and wall decorations of nightsticks and police shoulder patches from every department in the country. It was kept dimly lit so that you couldn't see the burst capillaries in the noses of its patrons or the tire tracks in the faces of the cop groupies who hung out in the place. The place was smoky, noisy, and crowded when we walked in, but it had probably been that way most of the day.

A beefy, big-faced detective looked up from his cluster of raucous companions at the bar and yelled, "It's the Bitch Goddess! Boetticher, come on over and join the celebration!"

We went over and Boetticher yelled over the laughter, "What's the occasion?"

"Remember that asshole who killed those two convenience-store clerks on Santa Monica two weeks ago?"

"Yeah?"

"Well, he ain't no more."

"Which brings up the eternal question," another cop shouted. "If a scumbag falls in East L.A. and there's nobody around to hear him, does he make a sound?"

Some loud philosophical debate followed, which Boetticher interrupted by asking the big detective, "You bagged him?"

"You bet your ass," the big cop said, and threw an arm around her shoulder and grinned. "And it's the most beautiful ass in the department."

She sloughed off the comment and bellied up to the bar. "A Wild Turkey on the rocks," she told the bartender.

"Two," Carlson said.

I was tempted to order a Pink Squirrel, just to see what the reaction would be, but said, "Three."

"What happened?" Boetticher asked.

The big cop had probably already told the story fifteen times today but seemed more than pleased to repeat it. "We got a tip he was gonna hit a 7-11 on Third, so Murphy and I set up a surveillance in the back of the store three days ago. We were starting to think it was all bullshit and were gonna call it when this morning at five-thirty the fucker shows up bigger than life. He just about cleared a sawed-off out of his coat when we blew him out of his socks. Shoulda seen that sonofabitch. Went through three aisles of Twinkies."

The group, which had all heard the story before, nevertheless responded with an appreciative explosion of laughter.

"I hope you read him his rights first," Boetticher said, deadpan.

The big cop looked momentarily troubled. "Now there it gets touchy. Some dickhead ACLU attorney might try to quibble and make an issue out of that. But hell, I think 'April fool, motherfucker' qualifies, don't you?"

There was an appreciative outburst of laughter and one of the crowd shouted, "You know the difference between catfish and lawyers?"

The beefy detective had the answer ready, "Yeah. One is a scum-sucking bottom feeder and one can breathe underwater."

The punch line drew more merriment from the raucous

group, and Boetticher had to shout to make herself heard: "Who was the guy? Anybody I knew?"

The big detective shrugged his large shoulders. "Who knows? Just another asshole. He had one of those nigger names. Like Santa Fe Offramp Jones."

Our drinks came and we hoisted them. Boetticher lifted hers toward the big man in salute and said, "Here's to another bad guy off the street."

"Hear, hear," the big man responded, and everyone lifted his glass.

Boetticher downed her drink all in one gulp, to the appreciation of the crowd. The big cop clapped her on the back and said, "The lady has balls. If we had more broads on the force like you, Boetticher, the city would be in better shape."

"I love you, too, Carozza," she said, putting her empty glass down on the bar. The big detective looked at me questioningly and she said, "Frank Carozza, Jacob Asch. Asch is a private investigator."

"PI, huh?" Carozza said. "Well, any friend of the Bitch Goddess is OK with me." Carozza turned to Carlson and his ebullience momentarily dampened. "Sorry to hear about your wife, Carlson."

Carlson acknowledged the remark with a nod. "Thanks."

I wondered what had happened to his wife. Whatever it was, it had instantly deflated the mood of the party and none of the cops protested when Boetticher said, "Let's get a table."

"I gotta go to the head," Carlson told her. "I'll find you."

We found an empty spot in a corner, wedged between a group of middle-aged, windbreaker-clad groupies scoping out that evening's prey, and sat down. We ordered three more Wild Turkeys from the cocktail waitress and I nodded toward the bar. "They seem to like you."

She smiled vaguely. "Only because they see me as an aberration. To most LAPD detectives, women cops are nothing more than secretaries with guns—incompetent at best, dangerous at worst. They see us as the unwanted flotsam of affirmative action."

"Why are you an aberration?"

"A lot of male cops are reluctant to get into a situation with a female partner, afraid they won't be able to handle it if the shit comes down. Unfortunately, it's true in a lot of cases. But my first partner trusted me. We were both on the same wavelength. We wanted the bad guys off the street. Consequently, we acquired a rep on the street for making the big busts. We took down a lot of guys. We even took out a few, to the consternation of the brass."

"Why is that?"

She shrugged. "Big cases, big problems. Little cases, little problems. No cases, no problems. A lot of cops forget that when they rise in the department. They become politicians susceptible to public pressure. And when you shoot somebody, there's always somebody around who'll scream police brutality. Bleeding hearts whose favorite play is *Les Misérables* and who think that these animals are regular people who just turned bad because they got a bad break somewhere, stole a loaf of bread because they are starving and are being hounded by the big, bad inspector. They don't understand that there are predators out there for whom life, property, and human dignity are nothing but something to take away from somebody else. And when you face off somebody like that, you've only got two choices: you take him down or he takes you down."

I pointed to the scar on her neck. "Is that where you got that?"

She nodded slowly. "My last bust in uniform."

"How did you get it? Or do you mind me asking?"

She took a breath. "My partner and I rolled on a silent alarm call at a jewelry store on Santa Monica. When we got there, we found the back door had been jimmied. We'd had a series of jewelry store burglaries in the area, same MO, back door jimmied, alarm tripped, but the guy had always gotten out before we got there. Smash and grab, in and out quick. The guy knew what he was going for.

"We didn't hear any glass breaking inside and we didn't know if anybody was still in there or not, so we drew our guns and went in. We found one of the glass counters smashed, so we figured we were too late again when all of a sudden this asshole stands up from behind another counter and *bam! bam! bam!* Fred went down and I started returning fire. It was like a dream. It all went down in a few seconds, but it seemed like some slow-motion scene in a Peckinpah movie. We were standing ten feet from each other, shooting at each other, then he finally went down."

"You killed him?"

"I thought I had. He looked dead enough. I reloaded another clip—I'd emptied my fourteen—and kept my gun on him while I went over. The asshole wasn't moving. I kicked the .38 away and bent down to get a pulse when suddenly he rolls over and I see this little .25 in his hand. Staring down that bore, I can tell you, it didn't look so goddamn little, especially when it went off. My neck was burning and I put two more rounds into the guy. I'll say one thing for him—he was one tough sonofabitch. I'd hit him with four 9-millimeter rounds, two of them in the chest, and he still had enough in him to come at me."

I tried to visualize her standing in the store, gun blazing like some female Wyatt Earp. The image was oddly arousing.

"What about your partner?"

"The first two shots hit him in the face. He was dead when he hit the floor."

There was something vaguely familiar about the incident. "I think I remember reading about it in the papers when it happened."

She nodded and her tone became cynically caustic. "Yeah, it made all the papers. And the six o'clock news. Fred was wrapped in a flag and given a fancy department burial, and I was billed by the brass as some kind of Wonder Woman.

The mayor saw it as a political opportunity to win the equal rights vote, and the chief saw a chance to get some badly needed good PR for the department, so they played it up in the media and promoted me to detective. First, Vice for a year, then Homicide. I feel funny about it sometimes."

"Why?"

"It was Fred's dream as well as mine to make detective. We busted our butts for it. It was just the luck of the draw that I lived to get it and Fred didn't. It could have just as easily been the other way around." Her expression darkened at the memory. "Funny thing, but the burglar who killed Fred was a scumbag named Leonard Dotson. We'd busted him for an armed robbery one year before, and he'd been sent up for five years, but some knee-jerk appellate judge overturned the case on a technicality. He shouldn't have even been on the street. If the system had done what it was supposed to, Fred would be alive today. Something is radically wrong somewhere."

"You like working Homicide?"

"A hell of a lot better than Vice. There's nothing morally equivocal about it, like busting hookers or arresting people for betting on a racehorse. You're dealing with the ultimate crime—murder. You're hunting people who steal from others the ultimate gift—life."

I liked listening to her talk, the throaty tone of her voice, the cadence. More than that, I liked what she had to say. There was a good mind under that well-molded steel exterior. "How long have you and Carlson been partners?"

"Ever since I came to Homicide. Five years."

"You like working with him?"

"Art's a good cop. One of the best. I owe him a lot. He taught me everything I know. A lot of guys would have resented being stuck with a woman partner, but not Art. He could see right away I had a brain and that I wanted to learn, so he showed me the ropes. He taught me what to look for at a crime scene and what to ignore. He showed me how to interrogate a suspect, how to coax testimony out of witnesses.

He treated me like a human being instead of just some skirt the mayor was using to kiss the ass of women's lib."

I hesitated. "I probably shouldn't say this, but he seems a bit . . . shaky."

She frowned sadly. "Art's been through a lot lately. His wife committed suicide a couple of days ago."

I immediately felt guilty for having shot my mouth off. "Jesus. No wonder."

She glanced past my shoulder and signaled me with her eyes to shut up. She looked up and said, "You found us."

Carlson pulled up a chair and sat down. He scanned the room with a sour expression. "What does somebody have to do to get a goddamn drink around here?"

"Take it easy," she told him. "They're on their way."

I felt sorry for the man and awkward at the same time. I wanted to offer my condolences, but Boetticher obviously didn't want him to think she had confided the matter to me. In a way, ignoring the issue was easier. I always felt stupid and clumsy offering sympathy to anyone who had just lost a loved one, especially someone I barely knew.

The waitress arrived and I paid for the round. Boetticher thanked me, and Carlson managed a half-audible "Thanks."

She entertained me with war stories from her career as a cop, and I listened enchanted, while Carlson brooded silently, knocking down three drinks to our one.

At one point, she made an obvious effort to get Carlson out of his doldrums by bringing him into the conversation. "Remember that time we went on a shooting call down in Watts? That little weasel dealer Walls got rained on over a burn bag?"

He lifted his head up with great effort and blinked at her, his eyes unfocused. "Yeah."

She turned back to me. "Here we are, me, Art, and two uniforms, standing around this guy on the sidewalk who has three .38s in his back, waiting for the ME boys to show up, and this crowd starts to gather. Pretty soon they start to get restless, talking trash to each other and us, and I start to get nervous thinking about what's going to happen if they get really brave and decide to go for our guns. I want to call in some backup, but old Art here just shakes his head and says, 'I'll handle it.' All those eyes are on him as he calmly rolls up his sleeve, takes the badge off his belt, and pushes the spike through his forearm and fastens it. Then he turns to the crowd and says, 'OK, anybody have a problem here?' That calmed them down real fast. They knew they were dealing with a total lunatic."

She laughed, but the trip down memory lane didn't seem to have improved Carlson's mood any. He murmured sullenly, "Fucking bunch of porch monkeys."

That depiction of Carlson as Mr. Macho, the teacher and leader, and Boetticher as the follower and student, conflicted with my impressions of the homicide team. She seemed to be the one in charge now. I wondered when and how the role reversal took place.

Boetticher looked over at her drunken partner with concern in her eyes. She said, "OK. Time to go."

Carlson's eyes left me and he blinked at her, trying to focus. "Go? Go where?"

"Home."

He shook his head. "I don'wanna go home. I want another drink."

He waved for the waitress, but Boetticher took his arm and said firmly, "You don't need another drink. Let's go home."

"It's lonely there," he mumbled sadly. He looked at her with a lascivious grin. "I will, though, if you come with me."

"Sure, I'll come with you," she humored him. "Up." She stood, and I marveled at her strength as she hoisted him to his feet.

I knew he was blitzed, but I didn't realize just how blitzed until he put one foot in front of the other, swayed like a palm tree in a hurricane, and had to grab the table to steady himself. I rose and grabbed his other arm, and together we braced him up, but he shook off both of our grips and straightened up in mock dignity. "I'm all right. I don't need any help."

He only bumped into three or four chairs on the way out, and Boetticher shrugged at me and we followed. He started to get behind the wheel, but she took the keys from him and told him to slide over, which he did. By the time we got out of the parking lot, he was snoring like a rhinoceros. I nodded at the drunken sleeper. "You and he have a thing going?"

"Me? And Art?" She laughed derisively. "Hardly. Art is like an older brother to me."

"You wouldn't tell by that look in his eyes."

She shrugged. "He's just drunk. He's lonely and feeling bad and wanted a shoulder to cry on, that's all."

"What are you going to do after you get him home?"

"I don't know. Go home myself, I guess."

"Are you hungry?"

She thought about it. "As a matter of fact, I am."

"I'll buy you dinner."

She took her eyes off the road for a moment to glance at me. "Where?"

"We can decide that after we deposit the load."

"We?"

"Sure. That way we can both work up a good appetite before we eat."

She smiled and said, "You're on."

She got on the Pasadena freeway, exiting into the hills of Highland Park. As she wound into the hills, the lowland *barrio* of rundown apartment buildings and small houses with yards littered with rusted bicycles and dead car carcasses metamorphosed into a semiaffluent, upper-middle-class neighborhood stamped WASP. After negotiating several rights and lefts, she stopped in front of a large two-story shingle-roofed house set into the hillside.

I started to get out of the car, but she turned to me and said, "I can handle it from here."

I pointed to the dozen or so steps leading up to the front door and asked, "Sure you're not going to need some help? Those steps look awfully steep."

She smiled. "I'm used to it. Anyway, he'll walk."

She got out of the car and opened the passenger door and shook Carlson violently. "Art! Wake up! You're home!"

He came awake and looked around groggily. "Huh?"

"Home!" she shouted. "You're home! Let's go."

She pulled him by the arm and he struggled out in a daze. I got out of the car to take his place in the front seat, but he didn't even seem to know I was there, which was OK with me. Taking him by the elbow, she led him up the stairs like a child. On the front porch, she took his keys from him and unlocked the door, and he said something and lurched forward clumsily, trying to put his arms around her. She took a quick step back and put both hands on his chest, warding him off. After a brief conversation, she patted him on the back, gave him a gentle shove through the door, and came back down to the car.

"Phew," she said, sliding behind the wheel.

"All I can say is that if his feelings toward you are purely fraternal, then incest must run in his family."

"I don't know what got into him," she said, shaking her head thoughtfully. "He probably won't even remember in the morning, and I'm not going to tell him. It'd only embarrass him and he feels guilty enough as it is without adding more to the kitty."

She started up the car and headed down the hill.

"You mean about his wife?"

She nodded. "He blames himself for her death."

"That's common in a lot of suicide cases. People feel guilty. They wonder what they could have done to prevent it. That's why a lot of people commit suicide—to make the ones they leave behind buy into it."

"There was nothing Art could have done. She'd been on that road for a long time. She tried once before. Almost made it. It was inevitable that she would succeed one of these times. Actually, it's probably better that she did. She made Art's life a living hell. He's been coming apart under the strain over the past year or so, hitting the bottle heavy. He talked about leaving her dozens of times, but he somehow never did. I'm not sure why not."

"What was her problem?"

"Not problem," she said. "Problems. She was a sick woman, totally paranoid."

"Paranoid? What about?"

"About everything. Everybody was plotting against her. Her family, Art. She would pop some pills and hit the bottle and throw a wingding and accuse Art of carrying on an affair with me. There was nothing he could say or do to convince her otherwise."

"If she ever saw him behave like he did tonight, I could understand her feelings."

"Art's never done anything like that before," she said. "That's what worries me. He's starting to lose it and I wouldn't want to see him lose his pension on top of everything."

"How did she do it?"

"Ate his automatic."

"Nice," I said.

She nodded. "They had an argument that day before he went to work. It was the same old tune. She screamed, accused him of carrying on an affair with me, and he snapped. Told her for the umpteenth time he couldn't take her bullshit anymore and that he was going to see a divorce lawyer that afternoon. We talked about it that day. He unloaded on me a lot. That was why Art and I got so close, actually. He would cry on my shoulder, tell me how unhappy he was, and how he had to get away from her, that she was driving him nuts. He never made it to the attorney that afternoon. He went home instead. Found her on the bed with half her skull missing."

That sort of memory was fresh enough in my mind, although fortunately I hadn't been married to Graves. That picture must be a hell of a big suitcase to carry around.

"Let's talk about more-pleasant things," she said.

"OK with me," I said. "What kind of food do you like?"

"Thai?"

"Love it. I know a great little place on Pico."

"Just point me," she said.

At the moment, I could think of nothing better I would have liked to have done.

Nineteen

She dipped one of the satay sticks into the dish of peanut sauce and took a bite. "Mmm-mmmm. This is scrumptious. I'm glad you suggested this place. I'm going to come back here."

I took a sip of wine and smiled. *Scrumptious.* I hadn't heard that word in years. The candlelight from the table danced in her eyes. "Now that we're having dinner together, 'Detective Boetticher' seems kind of formal. Do you have a first name?"

"Leslie."

"Leslie," I said aloud, testing the name in my mind. "I like it. It fits you."

She laughed. "Probably because it's both a woman's *and* a man's name."

"Not at all. You're a strong woman, but that doesn't make you masculine," I told her. "Besides, I'm not attracted to men."

She raised a speculative eyebrow. "And you're attracted to me?"

"Extremely."

She smiled slightly, but said nothing. It may have been an

illusion in the candlelight, but it seemed that a bit of color crept into her cheeks. She dipped another piece of beef into the dish of peanut sauce, and I chided myself for having unclean thoughts as she pulled it off the stick with her teeth.

"So tell me, Leslie, when did you decide you wanted to become a cop?"

She shrugged. "I don't know. I considered the fire department, but I don't like smoke, so I decided to apply to the academy." She smiled. "I've always had a compulsion to compete with men on their own terms. That's why I made the remark about my name. I think it was intentional on my father's part. He wanted a boy and he treated me like one, which was OK with me. I was a bit of a tomboy. I always picked the sports they said a woman couldn't cut it playing. While other girls were playing with jacks and dolls, I was over in the dirt lot shagging flies with the boys. I was usually better than most of them, too."

"What did your father do?"

"He was a foundry worker."

"So you grew up back East?"

She nodded. "Youngstown. The armpit of the universe. I hated it there. I also swore growing up that I'd get out the first chance I had. And I did."

"How old were you?"

"Twenty."

"And you came to L.A.?"

She smiled. "Doesn't everybody?"

"What'd you do before you decided to become a cop?"

"Oh, lots of things. Went to school for a while, worked as a waitress, tended bar. I even worked construction for a year, but I knew none of it was for me. Then I saw a recruiting poster for the force and I thought, 'Why not?' I knew immediately it was what I wanted to do."

"Compete in a man's world."

"It was more than that. Maybe I was naïve, but I wanted to do something where I'd be making a difference. Most cops do, I think. You come out of the academy all full of hope and confidence, thinking you're going to make the streets safe for everybody. Only it doesn't take long before you realize you can't change anything. The system won't allow you to. You arrest some dealer for peddling dope on the junior high school playground, and two hours later, he's back by the jungle gym, dealing. The system isn't being run by police, it's being run by lawyers and bail bondsmen, who are making the money off what we do. The more people we arrest, the more money they make by turning them loose. They aren't kidding when they call it a revolving door."

The system. Cops could never seem to stop talking about it. I might not, either, if I had to deal with it every day. "If you're so frustrated, why don't you quit?"

She shrugged and daubed a spot of peanut sauce off her lower lip with a napkin. "I may one day. For now, I can't think of anything I'd rather do. And every once in a while, you run into a situation where you *can* make a difference, and that helps keep you going. You crack a case and help send some sociopath to the joint for life, and the parents of the twelve-year-old girl he raped and murdered look at you with tears in their eyes and say, 'Thank you,'and it makes you feel good. You've restored their faith in an orderly universe, that there is still hope for a shred of justice in the world. Sometimes, it even restores your own." She paused reflectively, then smiled. "Besides, working Homicide, the overtime is good."

We both laughed at that.

"How about you?" she asked. "How'd you wind up being a private investigator?"

"By accident. I was a reporter. I got into a scrape and this is what I wound up with."

"What kind of scrape?"

"I was working the crime beat for the *Chronicle*. I wrote a story on a murder trial and put in some details about the murderers'motivations, which up to that time had been secretly guarded by the DA's office. The prosecutor was naturally interested in identifying the leak and went to the judge, who pulled me into court and demanded the name of my source. I refused to give it to him, so the old fart found me in contempt and sent me to county jail until I came across."

"Did you?"

"No."

"How long did you stay in?"

"Six months."

She shook her head in admiration. "That must have been awful."

"It wasn't a lot of fun."

"I don't know if I could have done that in your place," she said. "I probably would have told them."

"No, you wouldn't have. You're tough."

Something changed in her face. "Maybe not as tough as you think. Why didn't you go back to being a reporter when you got out?"

"There were political complications. The owner of the paper owed some favors to the powers that be. He promised me the *Chronicle*'s political and legal support and in exchange he wanted my notes. I knew he intended to turn them over to the DA, so I refused. He yanked his support and fired me."

"What an asshole," she said.

"You won't get any argument from me there," I said. "When I got out, I found he'd made some calls to save face. The word was out I was an instigator and had various substance-abuse problems and was totally unreliable. I couldn't buy a job. When an attorney friend called me and offered me a job as an investigator, I took it to keep eating. I've been doing it ever since."

"Do you like it?"

"It has its moments. Not a lot, but some."

"I've checked you out. Your reputation as an investigator is pretty good."

"I've been checked up on so much during the past week, all my friends are probably sick of hearing my name."

She nodded as if she understood. "Ever been married?" She flashed me a brief smile. "Maybe I should ask if you're married now."

"Not now. Once. A long time ago."

"What happened?"

"She wanted a better life than a reporter's salary could buy and she found it. She's married to a doctor now—a proctologist. She went to him to have some hemorrhoids removed and he immediately fell in love. I've often wondered about that. It's not exactly the stuff romance novels are made of."

She laughed. "I like your sense of humor. It's almost as sick as mine."

"It gets me through the day," I said. "How about you? You ever been married?"

She shook her head. "I don't know any man who could handle me for any length of time. I'm pretty headstrong." She ran a finger around the rim of her wineglass. "Sometimes I think I'd like to settle down, have a kid and a family like normal people, then I put it out of my mind. At least for now. Cops are bad marital risks. They've always got another lover and they always bring her home at night—the street. Makes it kind of crowded in the bedroom."

"Sounds like a lonely life."

"A lot of the time, it is." She thought for a moment. "Cops are a breed apart. It's hard for other—normal—people to relate to what we go through. They've never seen a kid whose mother has sewn his mouth shut because he talks too much or a wife whose husband bludgeoned her to death because she didn't do enough housework or a gas station attendant who got shot to death for a dollar sixty-seven and a can of STP. They don't live in the sewer twenty-four hours a day like we do. They might know it's there, but they don't wade through it and smell it and dream about it when they sleep under their fluffy down quilts at night. On this job, you see not only the worst people, you see the worst in the *best* people. It starts to get to you after a while, it changes you. You start to think everybody's slime, which isn't real conducive to sustaining a relationship."

"You could always marry another cop," I suggested.

Her expression changed and she said emphatically, "I would *never* get involved with a cop."

"Why not?"

"That'd just be doubling up on the problem."

The waiter came with pad thai and garlic chicken and vegetables and chicken in a hot chili paste, and we ordered another bottle of wine. We talked and ate and drank, and the more we did, the better I liked her. Her thoughts about herself were pure, confident, not uncertain and contradictory like many people's, including my own. She was aggressive, strong-willed, and independent, but those qualities did not detract from her femininity at all. In her world, they were simply survival traits. By the time we had finished the second bottle of wine, her face was suffused with a soft, romantic glow, and I was totally enchanted.

I asked the waiter for the check, and she said, "You think the two killings—Graves and Lexine—are connected, don't you?"

"You just can't help talking shop, can you?"

She shrugged. "Sorry."

"It's OK. To answer your question, yes, I do."

"How?"

"Some of the stuff in that storage shed is heavy. Graves wouldn't have been likely to have lugged it all out himself."

"You're thinking he had a partner."

"Right."

"And the partner killed him?"

I shrugged. "It could make sense that way. The two of them were in the middle of the job, something happens, Graves gets his floor show canceled."

Thoughts simmered behind her eyes. "And Lexine, being the lure to get you out of the office, would have known who the killer was. He had to get rid of her before she snitched him off."

"It's a possibility, at least," I said. But I was still troubled by the scenario.

She must have seen that, because she said, "But not one that you have a lot of faith in."

"How'd you come up with that?"

"The look in your eyes."

"You *are* a good detective."

"What bothers you about it?"

"The fact that Graves would have targeted my office for a job. There's nothing in there worth anything. He had to know that. He was in there."

"How about your files?"

"That's what the detectives on the case suggested."

"I know," she said.

That one took me by surprise. "You talked to them?"

"To Grabner. I wanted to know what your status was on the Graves killing."

"What'd he say?"

"That you thought you were cute, but that you weren't a suspect. I got the feeling he didn't care for you much."

"Believe me, the feeling is mutual."

She laughed. "Grabner is a jerkoff. Always was."

"You know him?"

She nodded. "We went through the academy together. He typifies the chauvinistic, condescending attitude of most male cops in the department. Unless he's trying to get into your pants."

"Did he try to get in yours?"

Her eyes smiled. "Once. A long time ago. We were in a bar and he made the mistake of trying a game of grab-ass. I warned him twice. The third time, I grabbed him by his nuts and squeezed them so hard he went to his knees. His drinking buddies all got a big kick out of it."

The image made me smile. "You must be real popular with him, too."

"Oh, yeah. So you can see, whatever personal observations Grabner has about you don't mean much to me." She paused. "So what's your plan?"

"I don't know. Try to find out who Brad is, I guess."

"The name on the tape?"

"Apparently he was supposed to meet Graves the day of the murder. And the time was about right."

She nodded. "It's a slim shot, but I'll run the name

through the computer, see what comes up. I'll also ask some guys in Burglary. Maybe one of them will know a Brad."

"I'd appreciate it," I said sincerely.

I paid the check and we left. She drove me back to my car. I got out and she remained in the car with the motor running. I came around to the driver's side and bent down. She smiled up at me. "Thanks for the dinner. I enjoyed it."

"Maybe we can do it again."

"I'd like to."

She reached up and put her hands on my cheeks and gently pulled my face down to hers. Our lips met and her tongue explored the inside of my mouth, and as the kiss deepened and intensified, her breathing became heavy and excited. She broke off the kiss and stared at me strangely. Her eyes seemed to be boring holes into me, probing my face. "I'll call you and let you know what I've found out."

My mouth was too dry to speak, so I just nodded dumbly. She put the car in gear and took off, and I stood on the curb and watched her taillights disappear around the corner, then got in my own car and drove home.

The service had three messages for me when I checked in, one from Maury Resnick, a criminal attorney I did some work for on occasion, and two from Schayes. I left the numbers by the phone for the morning, got undressed, and fell into bed, but the troublesome facts of the case and the memory of that good-night kiss conspired to keep me from sleeping, until I finally gave up and threw on a robe.

I went into the kitchen and made myself a stiff drink, took it back into the bedroom and tuned the tube into an old black-and-white movie, which was interrupted every ten minutes by voluptuous blondes and brunettes in tight dresses telling me how anxious they were to talk to me, just dial 1-900-HOTSIES. My dream girl was waiting for me right now. All I had to do was pick up that phone. After the tenth annoying pitch, I finally managed to drift off, wondering if the advertisers thought men were dumber than women, or lonelier, or simply stayed up later.

Twenty

My dream girl, a leggy, icy-blond beauty who looked remarkably like Detective Leslie Boetticher, was slowly shedding her clothes in front of me, when the sound of the alarm sent her scurrying, embarrassed, into the bathroom, scooping up her discarded garments on the way. I turned off the alarm and blinked at the clock. Eight-oh-five.

I dragged myself out of bed and padded into the bathroom hopefully, but there was nobody there. My dream girl had been just that, but then so was everybody's. After performing my morning ablutions and partaking in several cups of double-strength coffee, I made my calls.

Maury Resnick's secretary told me he would be in court all day and that she had no idea what he wanted to talk to me about, but promised to tell him that I'd called. I called Schayes.

"Homicide, Schayes."

"This is Jacob Asch. You called?"

"A couple of times."

"I didn't get the message until late last night."

"You should check with your service more often."

116

"I keep telling myself that."

"Maybe you'd better drop down here this morning."

His tone was coldly flat, and I suspected the reason for that. "I was intending to do that anyway."

"Uh-huh," he said skeptically.

"Say about ten?"

"I'll be here."

I got dressed and grabbed a twenty-ounce coffee and a muffin at an am/pm on my way downtown. There was considerably more activity than the other night when I walked through the hallowed portals of Homicide at 9:55. Typewriters clacked, pencils and pens scribbled as detectives scrambled to prove their worth and make the ten o'clock paperwork deadline. There was an old LAPD adage: No detective is worth his salt unless he can finish up his paperwork and be in a bar drinking by ten in the morning.

Schayes was at his desk but didn't seem to be in any particular hurry. He had a foot up on his desk and was sipping coffee from a dirty mug that said LAPD INVITATIONAL GOLF TOURNAMENT on it. He was in his shirt-sleeves, his brown sports jacket draped over the back of his chair. He nodded at me casually and waved the mug at a chair. I sat and asked, "Where's that wonderful warm human being you so fondly refer to as your partner?"

He shrugged. "Around somewhere."

"They always are."

He frowned. "Never mind about Grabner. You never got back to me about your files."

"That was because there was nothing in them to get back to you about."

His head bobbed forward and he pursed his lips as if he were giving that serious consideration. "What about the fact that you'd identified the woman you tailed as Graves' girlfriend? You didn't think I might be interested in that?"

I shrugged. "You're a detective. I figured you'd have already found that out." Almost as an afterthought, I added,

"Oh, in case you hadn't heard, she was found dead yesterday morning. Murdered."

He scowled. "I heard."

I tried to lighten the mood. "Thanks, by the way, for the restraint with the newspapers."

One of his eyebrows raised. "This how you show your gratitude? By withholding information?"

"I didn't *withhold* anything," I corrected him. "I'm not obligated to do your job for you, Detective, or to call you up every time I find out something. At any rate, the identity of the woman was right there in *your* records. You could have dug it up a hell of a lot easier than I did, so come down off the pulpit and get human. I came down here of my own free will to fill you in on what I've found out. You want to hear it or not?"

His birthmark seemed to redden, but that might have been my imagination. He didn't say anything for a moment, then: "OK. Let's have it. *All* of it. Everything you've found out in the last seventy-two hours, down to the minutest little detail."

I brought him up to date, and as he took notes, he seemed to calm down. When I told him about the phone message from Brad, his interest perked. He opened a manila folder on his desk and pulled out a piece of computer printout. "Bradford Warren Gilman, male Cauc, age thirty-four, born Baton Rouge, Louisiana. Six arrests, two convictions. One for possession of heroin and an IV kit, one for burglary."

"Brad?"

"It's a good guess. I had the same thought you did about Graves having a partner. I went through his jacket and made a list of all his known associates. On 3-7-'91, he was arrested for 484 PC—larceny. Arrested with him was Bradford Warren Gilman. They were pinched trying to unload a suitcase full of Rolex watches. The arresting officers thought the watches were stolen, but the charges were dropped later when it was determined that they were phonies."

"Got an address on the guy?"

"Grabner is checking on it now. He's also running Gilman's prints against those we found in your office."

"You might want to also check them against the stuff that was taken from the ULOCKIT storage locker."

His back stiffened in his chair and he glared at me. "It may come as a surprise to a supersleuth like you, but some of us dumb dicks do know how to paint by the numbers."

"I didn't mean to imply you didn't," I said. "In fact, I'm quite impressed by your efficiency. My suggestion wasn't offered as a slight, but only in the spirit of cooperation."

I wasn't sure if he bought that totally, but his posture relaxed. I pointed at Graves' folder. "Mind if I take a look at that?"

"What for?"

"Just curious."

He thought about it, shrugged. "I don't guess it'd hurt anything."

Since his burglary conviction in 1990, Graves had kept busy. He'd been arrested four times, for possession of stolen credit cards, possession of burglar's tools, possession of cocaine, and the larceny beef. In each case, the charges had either been dropped for lack of evidence, or "dismissed, no further explanation available."

"What does this 'dismissed, no further explanation available' mean?"

"Just what it says."

"There are a lot of them on there."

"That's the way the system works."

"Is it possible Graves was a snitch?"

Schayes snorted. "*All* these assholes are snitches."

Graves' first bust after his release from jail had been for possession of burglar's tools. I skimmed the arrest report. While on routine patrol, LAPD officers had noticed a green 1979 Ford Pinto with a dent on the passenger's side, which they knew from previous experience to belong to William Graves, a known burglar, parked in front of an apartment building at 1556 Norton Avenue. The officers initiated surveillance on the car and at approximately twenty-one hundred hours, they observed Graves walking out of the building. Upon observing the police car, Graves appeared to become nervous, arousing the officers'suspicions. Graves got into the Pinto and sped around the corner, failing to come to a complete stop at a stop sign in the process, and the police gave pursuit and pulled him over. A search of the Pinto's trunk revealed the burglar's tools, namely a jimmy, a set of lock picks, a glass cutter, and a rubber-suction-cup device for removing cut glass. Graves was read his rights and taken into custody. The report was signed by James Hill and Waverly Barker.

The pinch looked solid, at least as it was written up, yet it had been "dismissed, no further explanation available." Of course, it might have been recounted differently than it had gone down, and additional facts may have come to light during a subsequent investigation that led to the dismissal. I wrote down the officers'names and the date of the bust, then looked up to see my favorite detective coming across the room with a printout in his hand. Grabner glowered at me and asked, "What are you doing here, Asch?"

"My civic duty."

"Asch just brought us some information," Schayes said. "Looks like Gilman might be our boy. Asch was over at Lexine Woods'apartment yesterday with Boetticher and Carlson. There was a message on Graves'answering machine from a Brad." He ran down the rest of it, then asked, "Did they do a comparison yet with the prints they lifted from Asch's office?"

Grabner nodded. "No match. But that doesn't mean anything, unless he went in bare-ass."

"Send them over to Burglary at Hollywood Division, see if they match up with what they took from the ULOCKIT stash."

"Right."

"Graves wasn't wearing any gloves," I said. "He didn't even have any on him."

Schayes blinked at me, turned up a palm. "What's your point?"

"If they both went in to rob the place, why would one wear gloves and the other not?"

"We'll ask him when we find him," Schayes said. He turned to Grabner. "The computer spit up an address?"

"We got lucky. Gilman had been cited for a traffic violation just last week. Unsafe lane change. The address he gave the traffic cop was the Yucca Arms, 1015 Yucca Street, Hollywood."

I mulled that over. "Lexine Woods'body was found in a dumpster on Yucca."

Schayes nodded. "Yeah. Kind of a funny coincidence, don't you think?" He stood up and plucked the jacket from the back of his chair. "Let's go pay a visit to Mr. Gilman and see what he has to say about how he's spent the last few days."

I asked, "Mind if I tag along?"

Grabner sneered at me. "Yeah, we do.'

"Maybe it wouldn't be a bad idea," Schayes mused. "If Gilman was in Asch's office that night, his presence could put a little extra pressure on the asshole."

Grabner didn't look as if he liked the idea, but didn't say anything.

Schayes turned to me. "Just remember, keep your mouth shut. We'll do the talking."

"No problem," I said.

Twenty-one

I took my own car and followed them over to the Yucca Arms, a moldering six-story hotel with window screens that weeped rust down its paint-flaked sides. The sign above the entrance proclaimed proudly YO WILL LIKE OUR ROOMS. YO .

Plastic potted palms and three winos in sagging lounge chairs decorated the lobby. The winos turned their ruined faces from the soap opera on the television to watch us warily as we walked past them to the empty reception desk. Schayes rang the bell for assistance.

Mounted on the paneled wall to the right of the desk was a stuffed swordfish. The decorator who had picked it out was a genius. It was perfect for the place—the sword was missing. I pointed up at it and said, "Looks like there was a little bulldog in that one."

Neither of them smiled.

I was still staring up at it when the clerk, a beanpole who looked shrunken inside his wrinkled shirt, came out of the back, a cigarette dangling from the corner of his mouth. He looked at Schayes challengingly. "Yeah?"

Schayes flashed his badge. "Bradford Gilman. What room?"

The beanpole thought about it, then shrugged. "Forty-one."

"Is he in his room?"

The cigarette bobbed up and down as the clerk said, "I wouldn't know. I ain't his fucking keeper."

Schayes fixed him with a hard glare. "Are there phones in the rooms?"

"Sure. What kind of a joint do you think this is?"

"A storage dump for shit, that's what kind of joint I think it is," Schayes said. "I wouldn't call Gilman and tell him we're on our way up, if I were you, unless you want your dick slammed in the Penal Code book. That would fall under the classification of aiding and abetting."

The beanpole shrugged nonchalantly. "His beef ain't none of my business."

"Just leave it that way."

We walked away from the desk and Grabner asked, "Aiding and abetting what? We haven't got a warrant for Gilman's arrest."

"He doesn't know that," Schayes said.

The pneumatic elevator wheezed and groaned up to the fourth floor, and we stepped out into a narrow hallway that smelled of mildew and urine and frying lard. At the other end of the hall, a baby wailed loudly. I didn't blame it. If I lived here, I'd be complaining about my lot in life, too.

Forty-one was four doors down on the right. Behind the door, a radio was playing rock and roll. Schayes and Grabner deployed on each side of the door and Schayes knocked. The volume of the music remained steady. After a couple of seconds, Schayes knocked again, but there was no response. Schayes looked at Grabner, then tried the knob. It turned. He pushed it and stayed against the wall as the door swung open.

There was no sound from the room except for the radio. Schayes nodded at Grabner, drew out his gun, and walked cautiously into the room. I waited for a few seconds and, when no shots rang out, followed them inside.

The room was large and shabby. The faded red carpet was worn down to the thread in spots, the walls and ceiling were water stained. An unmade Murphy bed was pulled out of the wall and various items of men's clothing were strewn over the bedcovers and over the back of the single worn and overstuffed chair. There was a scuffed dresser and a louvered screen in one corner. Next to it was a nineteen-inch TV on a flimsy rollaway cart. The clock radio was on top of it.

Both men stood in the middle of the room, their guns still drawn and ready. "Gilman?" Schayes called out.

No answer. A breeze blew through the open window, billowing the gossamer curtain liners and bringing the smell of smog and the sound of traffic into the room. On the radio, some woman was singing about how nothing was the same when she returned home to Ohio. Down the hall, the baby continued to lament about the fairness of the universe.

Schayes'eyes scanned the room and landed on the bathroom door, which was cracked open. He walked over to it and gave it a nudge, peered inside. He stood there for a moment, holstered his gun, and waved Grabner over. I followed.

A man was sitting on the toilet dressed only in blue jeans. He was small and stringy, with a long, sharp face that ended everywhere in bony points. From his red-blond hair, I guessed he would have been pale complected, perhaps even freckled, but right now his face was a dark gray-blue, blotting out any freckles that might have been there. A leather belt was cinched around his bicep, and below it, a syringe hung limply out of his arm, which was as blue as the ornate dragon tattoo adorning his bare chest, and covered with track marks, a few of which were abscessed.

On the edge of the sink next to him was part of the man's "works," a screw top from a wine bottle with a wire handle wrapped around it and some cotton balls. I wondered if he had cared enough about his health to use a sterilized needle.

Grabner put his gun away and said, "I hear they get free shit in junkie heaven."

"Couldn't have been too long ago," Schayes said. "He isn't ripe yet."

"Gilman?" I asked.

"Probably, but we won't know for sure until we print him." He turned to Grabner. "Call it in. Then start knocking on doors, find out who knows Gilman."

"Right," Grabner said, and went out.

To me, Schayes said, "You, out."

I shook my head sadly. "See how you cops are? You use me, then discard me like an old shoe."

"Until we know different, this is a crime scene. The less people around to contaminate it, the better. Especially civilians."

He watched me start toward the door, then disappeared into the bathroom. I veered away from the door and went to the dresser, where I had spied something that caught my attention. On top of the dresser was a fat roll of twenties and a familiar key: ULOCKIT 26.

Schayes' peeved voice said, "I thought I told you to leave."

I turned around. "It doesn't look like you're going to have to wait for a print match on that locker."

He walked over, looked at the key, then at me, disapprovingly. "Did you touch anything?"

"Do I really look that dumb?"

"No dumber than the dozens of cops I've seen fuck up evidence," he replied testily.

I ignored that and went on, "There must be five hundred bucks there. He must have made a score recently."

I took two steps over to the screen in the corner and took a peek behind it. There was a small refrigerator and a table on which was a hotplate, a bottle of distilled water, a candle, and a condom out of which spilled a fine white powder. "Looks like this is where he did his cooking."

Schayes walked up behind me. "Yeah. A real fucking chef."

"Aren't you going to taste it to make sure it's heroin?" I asked, straight-faced.

Schayes shot me a look. "I saw one rookie who'd watched too much TV do that once. The vets just stood there watching him with amusement, then yelled 'Timber!' as the kid's eyeballs rolled up in his head and he fell like a tree." I'd have been surprised if Schayes had gone for it, but you never knew until you gave it a shot.

Grabner came in carrying a roll of crime-scene tape. He was accompanied by a disheveled, dark-haired man with wary bloodshot eyes and a seamed, leathery face. He was of indeterminate age, the ravages of alcohol having long ago obliterated the normal visual guidelines that go into making such an assessment. He wore a dirty sports shirt and black denims, which looked as if he had been sleeping in them for about a week. He reeked of cheap wine.

"This is Mr. Newsome," Grabner said, introducing the derelict with false formality. "He lives two doors down. He knows Gilman. Right over here, Mr. Newsome."

Newsome reluctantly followed Grabner over to the bathroom door and looked in. He turned around and nodded. "That's Brad, all right."

"When was the last time you saw Gilman alive?" Grabner asked.

The man ran a hand through his greasy hair and thought. "Yesterday, about two, I guess. He dropped into my room and we shared a little wine."

"Do you know if he had any visitors between then and now?"

"Nobody I seen."

"Did you know Mr. Gilman used narcotics?"

"Sure. Wasn't no secret. He'd shoot up in front of anybody." He wagged his head, then said with intense seriousness, "I told him that shit'd kill him one day. It's poison."

I wondered what he would recommend as a substitute, Kickin' Chicken or Ripple. At least they were slower.

Grabner said, "Thank you for your help, Mr. Newsome.

You can go back to your room now. If we have any more questions, we'll be down to talk to you."

Newsome left, and Schayes waved Grabner over to the screen. Grabner took a look and said, "Looks like a case of a hype who got his mix a little too rich."

"Unless somebody slipped him a hotshot."

"The lab will have to sort that out." Grabner went to the door and stretched a band of the yellow tape across it.

Schayes said, "I'll say it one more time, Asch: Out."

Grabner lifted the tape and I ducked underneath it and went out into the rancid hallway.

I wasn't likely to learn much hanging around there, so I took the elevator down to the lobby. The winos were totally absorbed in their soap opera and paid no attention to me this time as I walked past them. They were probably fascinated to listen to people with problems worse than their own. In another few minutes, the troops would arrive and they would be able to adjourn upstairs for a continuation of the show.

I drove over to Hollywood station to give Leslie the news. The desk sergeant told me she wouldn't be back for a couple of hours, that she was attending funeral services for her partner's wife, so I left my name and number and started to leave. I was stopped by a large item pinned to the bulletin board by the desk. Between a wanted poster and an announcement of the annual Robbery–Vice softball game on Saturday was a piece of paper on which someone had written with a felt-tip pen:

FUNERAL SERVICES FOR EDITH CARLSON
WILL BE HELD AT FOREST LAWN CHAPEL,
THURSDAY, 12 NOON. THOSE WISHING TO ATTEND
CHECK WITH CAPT. SAUNDERS.

Edith. The name of Archie Bunker's wife. The same name as Carlson's wife, who had truly stifled herself. The name of the woman who had set up an appointment for two o'clock on the afternoon a man was to be murdered in my office, and who had called to cancel at the last minute.

What had the woman wanted to see me about? Was it because of what Leslie had told me, that she was emotionally unstable, and had fantasized a backdoor love affair between her husband and his partner? Had she decided to kill herself and canceled in a fit of despondency, figuring, What the hell, I'm going to blow my brains out anyway, why waste the money on a private detective?

Of course, it could have just been a coincidence. It wasn't that common of a name, but there *were* plenty of Ediths in the world, and the one who'd called me might not have been Edith Carlson. But I didn't trust coincidences, and this case was already too full of them.

By the time I got over to Forest Lawn, the chapel services were over. A dark-suited attendant there gave me directions to the gravesite, and I wound my way slowly downhill, finally spotting the cars that lined the right side of the road. I pulled over and got my binoculars out of the glove compartment and focused them on the cluster of several dozen people congregated with their heads bowed, a quarter of a mile from the road. I moved the binoculars over the crowd, looking for Leslie. She wasn't hard to find. She would have made a nice addition to any funeral. Her long body was sheathed in a tight-fitting black dress and black nylons, and as inappropriate as it may have been, I could not help but feel a stirring in my loins.

I watched for a while, and then the priest said his la-de-dahs over the casket before it was lowered into the ground. As the coterie of mourners watched the remains of Edith Carlson disappear into the earth, Leslie moved over to Carlson at the edge of the grave and wrapped a comforting arm around his shoulder. The group began to break up and make its way back to the cars, and I started up my own and drove down the hill before I was spotted. There was absolutely no reason for me to be there, and I didn't want my presence to bother Carlson. At least not until I found out what was going on.

Twenty-two

$\mathbf{T}$he magazines on the lobby table were fanned out in a perfect semicircle, and I hesitated reaching for one, reluctant to break up the symmetry. I wondered if there was a service that did nothing but go around to various offices and rearrange the magazines after visitors like I messed them up.

"Jake, how the hell are you?"

I hadn't seen Glenn Dietrich for over a year, but aside from a little more gray around the temples and a touch more salt in his neatly trimmed mustache, he looked the same. He was meticulously dressed, in a light-gray tweed sports jacket, charcoal slacks, a pale blue shirt, and a yellow and gray paisley tie. He was tall and thin, with a large Teutonic nose and eyes that always seemed to be smiling, which, in his line of work—chief investigator for the L.A. County Coroner's Office—was unusual.

We'd known each other for a long time, ever since my *Chronicle* days, when he'd been a fledgling coroner's investigator and I'd interviewed him for an article I was doing on the death of a rather famous movie star who had forgotten to wear his drinking helmet and had fractured his skull taking a header down a flight of cement stairs. We'd bent an elbow or two since then, and although we didn't see each other often, the amiable feelings and mutual respect had remained intact.

I stood up and we shook hands. "What brings you down here?"

"I need a favor, Glenn."

"If I can, you know that."

"I need to look at a coroner's report on a recent death."

"How recent?"

"Three days."

"A case of yours?"

"Uh-huh."

"Let's go up to my office."

We went to the elevators, and as usual, I felt slightly uneasy on the ride up to the security floor. That floor, on which Glenn's office was located, was the one on which the autopsies were conducted, and it is nearly impossible to describe how bizarre a trip down that long hallway is. When the elevator doors open, you step out into a surreal world, an abattoir, a human junkyard, where the last vestiges of whatever a person had been ceases to exist with the first, deep cut of a scalpel, and a man is truly reduced to the sum of his parts.

But if it is the end of the line for all those who enter horizontally, it is the starting place for any homicide investigation. It is a place where the dead still talk, where an exclusive intimacy exists between the pathologist and the deceased, in which secrets are given up in unspoken whispers, secrets only the dead could know. . . namely, how he or she died.

According to statute, the office of the medical examiner in L.A. County was required to determine the circumstance, manner, and cause of all deaths in the county "other than natural," which constituted about one-third of the fifty thousand deaths within its jurisdiction each year. That usually made for a very busy day, and as we stepped out onto the security floor, I could see that today was no exception.

Gurneys were lined up along the wall, their inanimate cargoes patiently awaiting the disassembly line, and I tried not to look at their faces as I passed. I felt better when we got into his office and he closed the door.

He sat behind his desk and I pulled up a chair. I found myself staring at the paperweight on his desk, a plaster mold of a set of teeth that had been constructed from impressions taken off a piece of cheese found in the refrigerator of an elderly murder victim. When the suspect had been apprehended, the bite mark impressions had been instrumental in his conviction. When Glenn had gone to work for the coroner's office, he had been going through dental school, and that mold was dear to his heart. Whenever we'd been out in a bar and a woman with magnificent legs would walk by, Glenn would comment on her perfect dentition. A tooth man.

His voice jarred me out of my hypnotic state. "So what's the case?"

"Edith Carlson. A suicide. Gunshot."

He nodded. "The cop's wife."

"Right."

His eyes were still smiling. "I handled it personally because of the LAPD connection."

"And the official verdict is suicide?"

"That's right. It was pretty clear-cut."

"How clear-cut?"

He shrugged. "She left a note. She had a history of emotional instability and a substance-abuse problem. The morning she did the deed, she and her husband had a fight. He told her he was going to leave her. The same thing happened a year ago. That time, she tried it with pills."

"Women don't usually use guns. Too messy. They don't like to look bad, even in death."

"This time, I guess she didn't want to leave anything to chance."

"What was the fight about?"

"She accused him of having an affair with his female partner. According to Carlson, she was fixated on that idea."

"Think there was anything to it?"

"Who knows?" He grinned. "I couldn't blame him if it was true. You seen her?"

I nodded.

"Great teeth. The most beautiful incisors I've ever seen."

Next time I saw her, I'd have to take a closer look at her incisors.

He continued: "Anyway, it's doubtful. I talked to the shrink she'd been going to. He told me the woman was a paranoid personality. Borderline schizo. The husband apparently wasn't the only one plotting against her. Her mother, her sister, they were all doing stuff behind her back."

"Where was the husband when she did it?"

"At work."

"You verified that?"

"Yeah." He paused and eyed me curiously. "Who's your client, anyway?"

"Me."

"Huh?"

"A man was murdered in my office a few days ago while I was out. I'm trying to find out why."

"And this has something to do with it?"

"That's what I'm trying to determine," I said. "Is the coroner's report complete?"

"I don't know if the tox report is in yet, but the verdict is official."

"Would it be all right if I took a look at it?"

"I don't see the harm." He picked up the phone, pressed the intercom button and said, "Jane, I want the file on an Edith Carlson. That's right. The autopsy was done two days ago. Thanks."

We killed a few minutes with small talk, then a statuesque brunette walked in and handed him a folder. I looked at her retreating derriere and said, "Great bicuspids."

I turned my attention to the report. The autopsy had been performed by a Dr. Kodaka; his verdict was that Edith Carlson had died as the result of massive brain damage caused by a single gunshot wound to the head. The bullet had entered through the roof of the mouth and exited the top of the skull, cutting a path of destruction through the brain stem, the cerebral cortex. She had been thirty-seven years old, weighed 120 pounds, sixty-six inches in height, with brown hair. I tried to visualize what she had looked like, but the only image that came to me was a woman with half her head missing. There were no other signs of violence on her body to suggest the gunshot had been the end result of a struggle. Blood, vitreous humor, and urine, as well as her liver, kidneys, and spleen had been saved for toxicological examination, which had apparently not been completed yet. Determination: probable suicide.

"Isn't it kind of rushing things to officially list the death as suicide before the tox report is in?"

"Not when there's nothing to contraindicate," he said. "I looked at this one real close, Jake. Everything pointed to suicide. Her prints were on the barrel of the gun, as well as on the trigger guard and smudges on the grip. She held the barrel of the gun when she put it in her mouth and pulled the trigger with her thumb. There was gunpowder tattooing around her mouth and powder smudges on her hands. The direction of the blood splatters on her hands were consistent with her holding the gun."

I looked over the investigator's report. Following up a call to the coroner's office at 11:12 P.M., on June 21, the same night as Graves'death, the investigator, D. Burnett, had proceeded to the Carlson home in Highland Park, where he found Edith Carlson in the upstairs bedroom, dead from an apparent gunshot wound to the head. In her hand was a 9mm Beretta automatic, later determined to belong to her husband. She had been dead approximately four to six hours. On the table beside the bed was an empty bottle of chloral hydrate, a half-consumed fifth of Scotch, and a typed note, an apparent suicide message.

The rest of the account was mostly a recitation of events by Arthur Carlson. He and his wife had had a domestic argument at around 1:00 P.M., after which he had gone to work at

Hollywood station. According to Carlson, she had been drinking steadily since morning and was inebriated and emotionally upset. Upon his return from work at 11:00 P.M. he'd found her in the bedroom, after which he'd called police and the coroner.

There was a copy of the suicide note in the folder.

> Arthur—
> I can't go on any longer.
> You can have what you want now.
> Good-bye.

"She didn't sign the note."

He made a flippant gesture with his hand. "I guess she figured he'd know who it was from."

"You checked out the typewriter?"

"Of course," he said. "It was downstairs in the den. The type checks out."

"Did her shrink see the note?"

He nodded. "He said it was just the kind of note she would have left. She blamed everybody else for her troubles and she tried to unload on them the guilt and shame she felt because of her own low self-esteem."

"What about this empty bottle of chloral hydrate?"

He shrugged. "She had a script for them. Told her doctor she had trouble sleeping. But her husband said she was hooked on them. Her doctor verified that, too. He said she called him last week wanting a refill—said she'd lost the bottle—but he refused to give it to her. He'd just written her a script for fifty, two weeks ago."

While I digested that, his phone rang. He picked it up. "Yeah. Really? Hmmm. OK. I'll let them know." He hung up and shook his head. "We got a call from a woman yesterday, said her husband had died in his sleep. We went over, found him dead in bed. Thought he had a stroke. Looked routine enough. He had a history of high blood pressure, no signs of violence, but we gotta do an autopsy because it was an unattended death. That was the pathologist. He found a wound-track in the guy's brain, traced it out to a small hole in the side of the skull. The wound didn't bleed much and was covered by hair, so we missed it. Ice pick. Gotta call Homicide, let them know they have a murder on their hands."

"The wife?"

He shrugged. "That's their worry."

I put the report back on his desk. "When do you think the toxicology report will be in?"

"The preliminary should be in in a couple of days. We're short staffed because of vacations, and the lab's behind."

"Can I give you a call and check on it?"

"No problem."

We said our good-byes and I went out into the hallway. As I went toward the elevator, I passed an open refrigerator door. Inside, a black attendant maneuvered a forklift around inside a cavernous room in which plastic-wrapped bodies were stacked on fiberglass trays from the floor to the ceiling, a warehouse for the dead.

The old, the young, and the in-between, the dim-witted and the sly, the victims of violence and virulence, foolishness and despair, casualties of love affairs gone wrong and love affairs that never were, they all wound up here, to be flayed and emptied, quantified and qualified, drained and debrained, in an effort to reconstruct the last mysterious moments of their respective lives.

Before I mentally started to reconstruct my own, I quickened my pace and got the hell out of there.

Twenty-three

 I stopped at the Blue Whale and, between the salad and swordfish, used the pay phone to call the Hollywood station. Leslie had not returned. I took my time over dinner, ruminating on those events that alter and illuminate our times, then drove home.

I'd just turned on the tube and settled into the couch with a see-through when the phone rang. It was Leslie. "You dropped by today."

"Yeah. How was the funeral?"

"Depressing, like all funerals should be."

"How's Carlson holding up?"

"He'll be OK. I left his house a little while ago. He's getting drunk with his buddies." She paused. "Any special reason you dropped by, or was it just a social call?"

"Something came up I thought you might be interested in."

"How about if I drop by and you can tell me about it?"

That caught me off guard. "Now?"

"If it's a bad time—"

"No, no, it's fine. Where are you?"

"Five minutes from you."

136

"How do you know where I live?"

"You think you're the only detective around here, Mr. Asch?" Her laugh was rich and throaty as she hung up.

I gave the kitchen a crash cleanup and was being ever the optimist and running an electric razor over my face when the doorbell rang.

She was still in her funeral outfit. Looking at her almost made me want to crawl into a coffin. Her hair was pulled back and pinned with a wide black clip. "Hi."

"Hi," I replied glibly.

She looked at me uncertainly. "Am I disturbing you?"

"Not at all," I said, holding the door open for her. "Come in."

She stepped past me and I was caressed by the smell of her perfume. "I'm not in the habit of inviting myself over to men's apartments. But I was on my way home, and I didn't know if you'd come by about something important."

I closed the door. "Where do you live?"

"Manhattan Beach."

"Kind of a long haul to work every day, isn't it?"

She shrugged. "It's not that bad, really. And the sound of the ocean at night is worth the trip."

"I know what you mean. Can I get you a drink? I'm afraid all I have is vodka or bourbon—"

"Vodka is fine. No need to switch now. I've been hitting it since the funeral."

She held her booze well. I wouldn't have even guessed she'd been drinking.

I went into the kitchen and held up a rocks glass. "With?"

"Rocks. And a splash of water, please."

I made two drinks while she looked around. "Nice little place."

"Excuse its condition. The maid doesn't come until next week."

"You kidding? For a bachelor's pad, this is immaculate. You want to see a disaster, come over to my place."

I felt like asking when, but cooled it. No sense coming on

like a panting dog. I came around the counter and handed her
her drink. We sat on the couch and her nylons rustled as she
crossed her legs, exposing a good portion of perfect thigh.
She sipped her vodka, peering at me over the rim of the
glass. "So what did you want to tell me?"

"You talk to Grabner or Schayes today?"

"No."

"Ever heard of a Bradford Gilman?"

She inventoried her mind. "No. Why?"

"He was the Brad on Graves' answer machine. He was also
Graves' burglary partner. We found him this morning in his
room at the Yucca Arms. He was sitting on the can with a
needle sticking out of his arm."

She stopped drinking. "Dead?"

"As the minuet."

Her eyebrows knitted. "OD?"

"Looked that way. No signs of violence, and from the look
of his arms, he'd been mainlining for a long time."

She gave that some thought. "Think it's connected to the
other two killings?"

"I don't know," I replied truthfully.

"You said 'we' found him. Who was with you?"

"Grabner and Schayes."

"What else did you find there?"

"A dupe of Graves' ULOCKIT key. Other than that, I don't
know. I got the bum's rush."

"I'll call Schayes in the morning." She took another sip of
her drink and her mood suddenly lightened. She smiled and
said, "Let's not talk about it anymore. I'm off duty and I've
dealt with enough death today."

"What would you like to talk about?"

"Pleasant things," she said softly. "Like last night."

I swallowed hard. "What about last night?"

She put her glass down on the coffee table and leaned
close to me. Her breathing became irregular as her eyes fixated on my lips, and in an instant replay of last night, she put
her hands on my cheeks and pulled my face slowly toward

hers. Her mouth sought mine hungrily, her tongue probing, her teeth gently biting my lower lip, and I was ready to go on to phase two when knuckles sounded on the door. She pulled back and looked at me questioningly and I shrugged and got up.

I managed to keep from groaning as I opened the door and Jan said, "Hi."

"Hi."

I stood there, looking at her stupidly, and she said, "Well? Aren't you going to invite me in?"

"Not tonight."

She sensed my discomfort and her eyes narrowed on my face. She pushed the door open wider and moved past me into the room. Two steps in, she stopped and her mouth turned up at the corners into a sly smirk. "Oh. I didn't realize you had company."

Like hell.

She turned on a smile that had been dipped in plaster and said to Leslie, "I don't believe I've had the pleasure."

Leslie returned the smile. "Leslie Boetticher."

"Jan O'Connor."

They sized each other up like two pit bulls getting ready for combat, then recognition dawned in Leslie's eyes. "You're a TV reporter."

"That's right."

"You did that series on police corruption a few years ago."

"Oh, you saw that."

Leslie nodded, took a sip of her drink. "I saw it."

"What'd you think?"

"I think it was a hatchet job."

Jan's smile evaporated. "How was it a hatchet job?"

"How? It smeared the entire department and caused a lot of good cops to resign."

The tension in the room was becoming palpable.

"If they couldn't stand the heat, maybe they didn't belong in the kitchen," Jan retorted testily. "Are you a reporter?"

"LAPD Homicide."

"That explains your attitude." She snapped her fingers and pointed. "I remember you. You're that female Wyatt Earp who got shot in a gun battle in Hollywood a few years ago."

"That's right."

"That was right around the time my series aired, I remember." Jan's smile returned. "So what exactly did you find objectionable about the series?"

Leslie shrugged. "Exactly? It was filled with innuendo, hearsay, distortions, half-truths, and downright lies. That's for starters."

"There were some cops on the force at that time who disagreed with you. We had some of them on—"

"Sure. A couple of snitches with their own agendas. Disguised, so nobody could recognize them."

"We just aired the facts," Jan said testily.

Leslie's eyes widened. "Facts? Like that segment you did on the death of Jerome Carruthers, for instance."

"What about it?"

"Your reporting was so biased it was criminal. You made it sound as if Carruthers didn't commit suicide in his cell, that somebody murdered him, even though the coroner's office ruled the death a suicide."

Jan's eyes narrowed. "Carruthers was accused of raping an LAPD lieutenant's mother. Don't you think it's kind of funny that the closed circuit camera in his cell was the only one in the entire jail that was turned off for a half hour? Precisely the time he hung himself?"

Leslie put her drink down. "If I remember correctly, you neglected to mention the fact that the lieutenant in question was not even on the premises at the time."

"He had plenty of friends who were."

"Oh, yes," Leslie said derisively. "The great conspiracy theory. The entire department was in on it. Everybody knew and everybody covered it up. Too bad you couldn't find one person to talk about it."

Jan shrugged. "I think people got the point."

Leslie leaned forward. "What point is that? That TV reporters are conscienceless, opportunistic scumbags?"

Jan's lips compressed and her face flushed with color. "No, that LAPD was corrupt."

The escalator of emotion was speeding up. Before somebody got tossed off, I stepped in front of Jan and said, "I think you'd better leave."

That seemed to cool her down. She shrugged and turned her icy smile on me. "OK."

I walked her to the door, and she paused and looked straight at Leslie. She forced a smile and looked up at me. "Glad to see you finally found your whore."

I pushed Jan out and closed the door before I had to start swabbing up bloodstains, then turned and grinned sheepishly at Leslie. "Sorry about that."

"You didn't tell me you had a girlfriend."

"I don't."

"It didn't sound as if she knows that."

"She's just a friend, really."

"She's a bitch."

"I can't argue with you there."

"She's lucky she left when she did. She would've looked funny doing the news with no teeth." She shook her head and stood up. "Maybe I'd better go."

"Why? Because of that?"

She shrugged. "I don't really know why I stopped over here."

"Yes, you do." I went to her and kissed her scar.

"What...what are you doing?" she said, but leaned her head back, exposing the nape of her neck to me. I touched my tongue to the scar, licked the circle of dead tissue, and she groaned, far back in her throat.

I pulled back and stared into her eyes. "Do you really want to go?"

"No."

"Then don't."

She thought for a moment, then unclipped her hair and

shook it loose. She took a step back, reached behind her and unzipped her dress and let it slide to the floor. She took her mourning seriously. She wore a black bra and panties, and a black garter belt held up her black nylons. Few women look better undressed than dressed, but she was one of them. Her stomach was flat and muscular, her breasts were firm and high, her long legs were slender but strong. My mouth went dry looking at her.

She sat back down on the couch and kept her eyes on me, watching me watch her as she slid a hand into her panties and began playing with herself. I kneeled on the floor in front of her and pulled them off, and my tongue took the place of her fingers. She moaned and pushed herself hard against my mouth, then suddenly, she pushed me onto my back on the floor and began frantically tearing at my zipper.

She pulled off my pants and mounted me and slid slowly up and down, growing more liquid with every movement, her eyes fastened on mine. She picked up the pace, moaning louder as I thrust deeper and deeper into her until suddenly she screamed and began to buck and thrash, seemingly losing muscular coordination as she approached orgasm. Her whole body was wracked by spasms as she came, and she threw her head back and let out a stream of obscenities and then I exploded in her and was soaring, lost, drifting.

She rolled off me and we lay on our backs on the carpet, soaked with sweat and slowly regaining control of our breathing.

"You probably think I'm horrible," she said after a while.

"That adjective is so far removed from what I think of you, it's ridiculous."

"I just don't believe in being hypocritical. I knew when I came over here tonight this was going to happen. I knew last night."

"I didn't, but I hoped."

"How about another drink?"

I took our glasses into the kitchen and made two more while she resumed her place on the couch. She looked up at me as she took hers and asked, "Would you mind if I stayed the night?"

"I was counting on it."

"Good," she said with a twinkle in her eye. "Because it's going to take that long to try out some of the things I have in mind."

I took her by the hand and led her toward the bedroom. "I have a feeling I'm going to like the way you think."

And I did.

Twenty-four

I was roused from a short, exhausted slumber by kitchen sounds and the aroma of coffee brewing. I cracked one eye and aimed it in the direction of the clock. Eight twenty-five.

I swung my feet out of bed, yawned and scratched, and padded naked to the door. She was standing in front of the gurgling coffee maker dressed in my black terrycloth robe. At least it hadn't been just a dream.

"Good morning."

She turned and smiled. "Good morning. Coffee's just about ready. How do you like it?"

Aside from a very slight case of pillow hair, she looked as perfect and unruffled as she had last night, before the blitz. I'd stumbled onto Wonder Woman. I just hoped she hadn't brought her magic lariat; then I'd have to confess how good she made me feel. "Cream and one sugar."

"Coming right up."

I took a quick, hot shower, and when I stepped out, a steaming mug of coffee was sitting on the sink. A man could get used to this, I thought. I pulled on my white robe and I worked on the coffee while toweling off, then went out to the living room where I was greeted by an early-morning surprise.

Leslie was seated at the breakfast table and the smile was gone from her face, replaced by a furrowed scowl of displeasure. The reasons for the change in her mood were instantly obvious. Across from her at the table, sipping coffee, were Schayes and a smirking Grabner.

"Morning," Schayes said. "Detective Boetticher here was good enough to invite us in for a cup of coffee. Care to join us?"

I frowned. "On the job kind of early, aren't you?"

"Yeah, well, like I said, we're dedicated public servants. We take our job seriously." Schayes took a sip of coffee, smacked his lips, and smiled appreciatively at Leslie. "Good coffee."

I poured myself another cup and stood at the counter. "I assume you're here for a reason."

Schayes nodded slowly. "We have some news we thought you might be interested in. Detective Boetticher, too. Actually, it's convenient for us we found you both together. Saves us telling it twice."

The smirk had not left Grabner's face. "We haven't told her yet. We thought we'd wait until you got out of the shower." He glanced over at her and dirty thoughts danced in his eyes. "I didn't realize what a personal interest she'd taken in this case."

Leslie did a knife-throwing act with her eyes and her voice was cold steel: "My personal life is none of your fucking business."

The smirk turned crooked and he shook his head. "Tsk, tsk. Is that any way to talk to a fellow officer?"

"Enough of that crap, both of you," Schayes said sharply.

"What's the news?" I asked.

Schayes said, "We're closing the book on the Graves killing. Lexine Woods, too, from the look of things."

"Why? What happened?" I asked.

"Remember we found no wallet on Graves in your office?"

"Yeah?"

"We found it in a bureau drawer in Gilman's room. There was a nice wad of dough in it, enough to keep Gilman high for a couple of weeks."

"He only had three hundred and fifty bucks on him when he came to my office. He cleaned out his wallet when he gave it to me."

"Maybe that's what he wanted you to think. He beat you for the hundred and fifty, remember?"

"Why would he pay me at all?"

"To get you out of the office."

"You ever heard of a burglar paying his victim to leave the premises? And why not just wait until nighttime, when they knew I wouldn't be around? Why would they take the chance of being seen in broad daylight breaking into the place?"

"Because they were stupid. Who knows what takes place in a couple of minds like Graves' and Gilman's? Frankly, I don't care. All I know is the evidence backs up that's what happened."

"What evidence? A wallet?"

"Not just a wallet," he said. He paused, I presumed for effect. "We also found the murder weapon. It was under Gilman's mattress, a .38 Smith and Wesson revolver. Firearms comparison has positively matched it up with the slug taken from Graves. And it had Gilman's prints all over it. Only Gilman's."

Grabner said, "The gun was registered to a Samuel Jenkins, of West L.A. He reported it stolen with a bunch of other stuff from his office four months ago. Some of the rest of the stuff has been identified in the stash from ULOCKIT."

Leslie asked, "What about Lexine?"

"In the bureau with the wallet was a coil of clothesline,

real similar to the kind used to strangle her. The lab boys are working on it now to determine if it's the same stuff."

Her eyes sparked angrily. "Why didn't you call me? Woods is *my* case—"

"Keep your robe on," Grabner said. "It's still your case. Nothing's been released yet. The lab results aren't even in."

She glared at him hotly, and I jumped in: "What about the cause of death for Gilman?"

Schayes shrugged. "Tox isn't in yet, but the preliminary results are OD. The shit he was shooting up was almost one hundred percent pure."

"When are they figuring he died?"

"Sometime between midnight and dawn the night before last."

"Accidental?"

"Suicide, accident, what difference does it make? Stuff that pure, it wouldn't have taken much of a dose to send him to la-la land. All I care about is it wasn't murder."

"You're sure about that?"

"The coroner's satisfied, I'm satisfied," Schayes said. "Personally, I think it couldn't have ended any more perfectly. A burglar, a hype, and a whore, all wrapped up in one neat package. End of mystery."

"Is it?" I asked. "What was Gilman's motive for murdering Graves?"

Schayes shrugged nonchalantly. "Maybe they had a beef, maybe they didn't like each other. Maybe Gilman was tired of splitting the spoils. Maybe he just wanted a fix and decided to take it from Graves. Who gives a shit? This isn't fucking TV, Asch. Motives are for lawyers and 'Murder She Wrote.' This goddamned case isn't going to court. All I care about is facts and evidence. And the facts are Gilman capped his partner, then had to do Woods because she knew about it. Over and out."

There was another LAPD adage: the primary goal of a good homicide detective is to find a way to turn a homicide into a suicide, so that it would go into the books as solved.

The incentive was political. If the homicide clearance rate was high, the department got praise and funding from the board of supervisors and the city council, lieutenants and sergeants got promoted, and pressure on detectives like Schayes and Grabner remained at a minimum. They weren't transferred back to Vice or Narcotics or Forgery in Norwalk, where they would have to commute seventy miles a day to work, and they were allowed to continue to do their jobs with a minimum of interference, which meant they could still be drinking with the boys at Little Joe's at ten every morning. I could understand it. If I were in their shoes, I might play the game the same way. But I wasn't in their shoes and it irritated the shit out of me.

"Don't you think it's pretty convenient, the guy keeping all that evidence around that would put him in the gas chamber, then knocking himself off like that?"

Schayes rubbed his birthmark and his voice took on an edge: "Yeah, I do, in fact. I think it's convenient for everybody. Me, Boetticher here, the DA, the taxpayers who don't have to pay for a fucking trial. In case you don't realize it, it's convenient for you, too. You're off the hook."

"I didn't realize I was on one," I said.

He stood up. "This was a courtesy call. I just thought you'd like to know. Next time, I'll let you learn about it from the papers."

"I appreciate the visit, Schayes."

Grabner rose and stared right at Leslie. His grin grew wider and he said, "The trip was worth it. A lot of guys are going to lose money on this one. There's a lot of bucks down that you didn't do it at all."

Leslie stared up at him with disdain. "When you're home making it with your soul mate tonight—your right hand— you can fantasize about it."

Grabner's smile faded, his face colored. "Go to hell, Boetticher."

Her lips twisted into a wry smile of her own. "I will, Grabner. So will you. But by the time you get there, I'll be running the gate."

Boetticher 2, Grabner 0.

"Thanks for the coffee," Schayes said quickly, sensing the hostility thicken. He tugged Grabner's elbow. "Come on."

As soon as the door closed, she sighed heavily and shook her head angrily. "That asshole. By tomorrow, I'll be taking male-locker-room shit from every cop in the department."

"Sorry."

"It's not your fault," she said. "I shouldn't have answered the door, but you were in the shower. Ah, what the hell. I've had it dished out to me for years. I can handle it." She glanced at her watch. "I'd better get going."

She disappeared into the bedroom and I sat at the breakfast table and had another cup of coffee. By the time I'd finished it, she emerged dressed. I walked her to the door and she turned and kissed me gently on the lips. When she pulled back, her eyes were intense. "I'm glad I stopped by, in spite of Grabner showing up."

"So am I."

"Will you call me?"

"Nothing could stop me."

She kissed me again and went out, and I watched her go down the stairs, then went back inside. I poured myself another cup of coffee and sat at the table and stared out the window at the whiteness of the daylight, and thought troubled thoughts.

Twenty-five

I got dressed and drove to the office and called the service. Maury Resnick had called back, also Jeff Schindler, another attorney, this one civil, who used my services on occasion. I called back Maury first.

His secretary told me he would not be in until later that afternoon, but he'd wanted her to convey to me his wish to employ me on an attempted murder case he was handling. I told her I would talk to him later about it, but that he could consider me on the meter as soon as I dropped by to pick up the case file, sometime this morning. Jeff Schindler was in. He also had a case he wanted me to work on, a civil suit he was filing against Westside Hospital on behalf of a client who had recently had surgery there. I told him the same thing I'd told Resnick's secretary and hung up.

Business was beginning to perk up. With the three unfinished conservatorship cases, I'd have enough work to keep busy for a while. Too busy to devote to freebie cases like the Graves killing, which was closed, anyway. There was no reason to go on with it. The only reason I'd gotten involved in the first place was because of the damage the publicity could have done to my reputation, and that was under control. The cops had their answers and were satisfied, so just drop it and get on to something that *paid*.

It didn't really matter if their answers were the right answers. I could understand their motives. You punch the name of a dead man into the computer, and it spits out a list of offenses against society that would paper the bottom of an eagle's cage and apathy sets in. People like Graves weren't victims, they were predators, so who gave a shit if they got blown away or where? When you could close out a file on a case like his, you did it. There were other victims out there— *real* victims—to be avenged, so why waste time on garbage like Graves?

Schayes had said it: a burglar, a druggie, and a whore, all tied up in a nice, neat package. So what if it was too neat? What was it to me? I was home free. I'd skated through it relatively unscathed. So my pride had been hurt a little. So I'd been taken in by Graves and my own cupidity, so what? Pride, after all, was one of the Seven Deadly Sins, and a luxury I could not really afford, especially right now when the rent was coming due. Follow the professionals' lead and drop it, Asch. If Graves had suckered you, he'd paid for it in spades, with the ultimate gift he could give, his life. What difference did it make that it was in your office or in the alley downstairs or in his own bed?

But the incontrovertible fact was, it *did* make a difference to me. I felt violated, exposed. Graves had been killed right here, in this chair. Behind my desk. Where I was now sitting. Dust eddied in the striated shafts of sunlight that streamed in through the venetian blinds and fell on the empty chair across the desk from me. I stared at the chair, then looked down at my hands on the arms of my own chair. Suddenly, it hit me like a jolt of electricity.

I'd been asking myself the wrong question all along. Instead of wondering what Graves had been doing in my office, I should have been asking myself *where* in the office he'd been when he'd been killed. I snatched up the phone and called Homicide.

Schayes wasn't in, so I left word for him to return my call and tried Hollywood Division. Carlson, I was told, had called in sick, and wouldn't be in today. I locked up the office and went down to my car.

I drove over to Santa Monica Car Rental on Fifteenth, where I got a rate on a green Subaru, and after transferring the gear I would need from the Mustang, I proceeded to West L.A, where I picked up the case files from Schindler and Resnick. It was a little after noon when I pulled off the Pasadena freeway and headed into the hills of Highland Park. My memory false-started a few times, but after wandering around for fifteen minutes or so, I found the house. I drove by and wound up the hill and parked behind the house on the street above. I slid over to the passenger side of the car and trained my binoculars down the steep, weedy hillside.

There was no residence above the house, and I had a clear view into the swimming-pooled backyard, but that was all I had. The shingled eaves of the roof obscured any view into the house, which meant I could sit here all day and never have any idea of what was going on inside. I ran my binoculars over the roof. The house was even bigger than it appeared from the front, another wing angling off toward the back of the sizable lot. This was not Beverly Hills—the neighborhood was racially mixed, and prejudice acted to keep property prices reasonable—but it was still a very nice house, especially on a cop's salary.

The day was quite warm and I was beginning to sweat. I watched the backyard some more. I killed time reading about the two cases I was now getting paid to investigate.

Resnick's client was one Philip K. Brodsky, a con man who had been arrested and charged with four counts of fraud and larceny after he had been turned in by one of his female victims. According to the charges, Brodsky had preyed on female immigrants by telling them over the phone that he was a "doctor from a federal clinic," and that they had been found to be carrying a rare disease that would require their deportation if not treated. The "treatment" was that the "doctor," Brodsky, would have himself injected with a serum, which could then only be passed to the victim through sexual intercourse. For this special service, the women only had to pay Brodsky $650. A search of Brodsky's apartment had turned up a white doctor's frock, as well as a list of names and addresses, including that of the woman who had come forward to police. A check of the list resulted in three other women saying they had been similarly sexually swindled, but investigators speculated that Brodsky's list of victims was considerably longer than that. Brodsky, a used-car salesman who had a record for running other bunco games, proclaimed his innocence, saying it was all a case of mistaken identity.

In the civil suit, the plaintiff, Amos Welk, was suing Westside Community Hospital because they had "recklessly and carelessly set fire to his buttocks" while performing routine hemorrhoid surgery. According to Welk's statement, the sterilizing alcohol they had been using had been ignited by a cauterizing instrument, causing second-degree burns over forty percent of his ass.

Ah, the glamorous life of a private eye, listening to senile old farts discuss the state of the union, interviewing immigrant women who spoke English about the strange way medicine was practiced in the U.S.A., and gathering statements from hostile hospital staff about haywire hemorrhoid surgeries and blazing booties. What the hell, it was money, which was more than I was getting on this job. I put the files away and went back to watching the house.

Several cars drove by, the occupants eyeing me curiously. I debated whether to stick around. I didn't even know if Carlson was inside, and if he was, he was probably sleeping off a hangover from his wife's wake. On the other hand, if one of the neighbors called the cops, Carlson would undoubtedly hear about it, something I definitely wanted to avoid. The debate was still ongoing when I heard a car engine start up and a red sports car backed out of Carlson's driveway. I slid over and fired up the Subaru.

We drove down the hill and I stayed far back until the sports car pulled onto the freeway. Traffic was not bad and I sped up, weaving in and out, all the while keeping cars in front of me as a shield. Finally, I worked up close enough to get a look at the car.

It was a new Dodge Stealth, sleek and shiny, but I couldn't get close enough to make out the license number. The lone person in the car, the driver, appeared to be a man, but I couldn't tell if it was Carlson or not. I dropped back and pulled two lanes over, trying to keep in his blind spot. Traffic slowed when we hit the downtown interchange, and when he pulled off onto the Santa Monica freeway without signaling, I attracted some angry horns as I cut off several drivers trying to get over.

Traffic on the freeway was bumper to bumper, and it took a good twenty minutes to get to the La Cienega exit, where he signaled and got off. I followed him up into the barren, scrub-covered hills covered with green cricket pumps that resembled prehistoric insects, their heads bobbing as they pierced the earth with steel probosci, sucking out of the ground the low-grade liquid remains of our distant dinosaur cousins. At Slauson, he took a right and drove past the upscale houses of Ladera Heights, and a few miles later, he pulled into the left lane for the Marina freeway as the light turned red. No other cars were signaling for the turn, which meant that if I wanted to stay on him, I would have to pull up directly behind him, something I really did not want to do. I pulled over to the curb a block back and kept my eye on the light, waiting for the left-signal arrow. There was a chance I could make the light before it changed to yellow, but I wasn't banking on it, especially with the pickup the rental didn't have. I reached for the binoculars on the front seat, thinking that at least I could get the Stealth's license number, but a light blue Honda pulled into the turning lane behind him, blocking my view.

The light changed and I tossed the binocs back onto the seat and punched it. The Subaru careened across three lanes of traffic, and I sailed through the intersection just as the yellow arrow flashed.

He drove fast and I had to keep the Subaru floored just to keep the Stealth in sight, but a few miles later, the freeway ended and I was able to close the gap. At a sign for Marina del Rey, the Dodge made a left, and just before Lincoln, he pulled into the parking lot of a coffee shop with a huge Dutch-style windmill out front. As I passed, the driver was opening the door of the Stealth, but I could not get a good enough look at his face to see if it was Carlson, and if it was, I didn't want to slow down too much to risk him getting a look at me.

I turned onto Lincoln and pulled into the driveway on the other side of the restaurant and found a space from which the Stealth was visible. I could see the back bumper of the car, and I tried to get a look at the license plate with the binoculars, but the angle was bad. I thought about trying to get close enough on foot to get a look but decided the risk wasn't worth it. I'd just have to wait for another chance.

Half an hour later, a man came out of the door of the restaurant and walked over to the Stealth. I trained the binoculars on him while he opened the door. It was Carlson. He was wearing an orange windbreaker, jeans, and running shoes. He got into the car and backed out of the space and pulled out of the driveway onto Mindinao Way.

He took a left at Admiralty and a right on Fiji Way, a tree-lined finger of land that ran into the marina, where an armada of pleasure craft bobbed picturesquely. He pulled into the parking lot of Fisherman's Village, a collection of brightly painted shops and restaurants, all done in gable-roofed, pseudo–Cape Coddish style, anchored by a fake lighthouse at one end. I pulled over while he took a ticket from the automated parking gate.

He parked the car and went into a store whose distressed wood sign read BRAUTIGAN YACHT SUPPLY. The parking machine spit a ticket into my hand and I drove through the gate, picking a space on the far side of the lot. Carlson came out of the building ten minutes later, carrying a large brown paper bag. He put the bag in the car and took off.

By the time I'd paid the cashier-thief in the kiosk seventy-five cents for my ten minutes of parking, Carlson was making a left onto Admiralty. I sped up and made my turn in time to see him turning left again, at Mindinao. Half a block down, he pulled into the lot for pier 44 and parked next to Harpoon Harry's, one of those trite, wharfy-barfy restaurants that looked like an abandoned tuna cannery, with collapsed wood walls and a corrugated tin roof. I drove to the end of the street, turned around, and made another pass of the lot.

Carlson was out of the car, his bag cradled in his arm, unlocking the security gate across one of the pontoons that moored cabin cruisers and sailing craft of various shapes and sizes. I pulled in and parked a few stalls away from the Stealth and focused my binoculars on Carlson, who was through the gate and walking down the pontoon.

I pulled into the lot, parked in front of the restaurant, and focused the binoculars down the pontoon. Forty yards down, he stopped and stepped aboard a boat, my view of which was blocked out by a huge cabin cruiser moored in front of it. I trained the binoculars on the number on the pontoon gate. C6.

I considered my options. The marina office was only twenty yards away, to my right, and I couldn't sit here for very long without attracting somebody's attention. Harpoon Harry's, on the other hand, might afford a better view. It was on the water, and from its front windows I would have a good view of the pontoon. It would be a hell of a lot more comfortable, and I could get a drink and some lunch if Carlson stayed aboard ship long enough. My stomach growled, seconding the motion, and I picked up the cassette recorder and locked up the car.

As I walked by the Stealth, I looked at the license and intoned into the recorder: "Two twenty-two P.M., December eighth, subject entered gate C6 of pier 44, off Mindinao, Marina del Rey. He's driving 1991 Dodge Stealth, California license number 2GU435." I pocketed the recorder and went through the doors of the restaurant.

The front of the place was a large bar and lounge, filled with captain's chairs and wood-barrel tables. Stairs led down into the large dining room, the decor of which remained true to the exterior's dilapidated-cannery theme. It was all distressed wood, with a high, barnlike ceiling crisscrossed with exposed air-conditioning ducts. Round, green lamps hung down on long cords from the ceiling, throwing their light on tanks of tropical fish and live lobsters living out their last days on death row. As I suspected, the entire front of the restaurant was glass, so that patrons could gaze out at the ships huddling in the marina, their rows of sheathed masts looking like a forest of leafless, bright blue trees.

There were only a few late lunchers in the place, and I asked the ponytailed blond beach-bunny at the front for a booth by the windows. I picked one with a good view of the pontoon and ordered a Lite beer from the waitress while I looked over the menu. When she came back with the beer, I ordered the sole meunière and a salad and settled down to wait.

The boat Carlson had gone onto was still obscured by the big boat in front of it, but I had a clear view of the gate that he would have to come through when he left. I nursed my beer and poked through lunch, which tasted as if it had been caught before the cannery had been abandoned.

An hour and twenty minutes later, Carlson still hadn't shown, and except for me, the dining room was deserted. My waitress explained she was going off shift and asked if she could close out my bill. I gave her cash, threw in a twenty-percent tip, and asked if I could keep drinking at the table. She informed me that the bar was open, but I flashed her a big smile and said very pleasantly that the view from the booth was so nice I preferred to stay put, and she shrugged indifferently. I ordered another beer from her replacement—

a fishnet-stockinged, gum-snapping cocktail waitress, who did not try to conceal her annoyance at having to make all those extra steps from the bar—and kept my eyes on the window.

At 4:10 Carlson came walking up the pontoon and I got up and headed for the front of the restaurant. I'd just about made it when, to my consternation, I saw Carlson coming through the front doors, heading right for me. He stopped and turned to shake hands with a man standing just inside the entrance, and I put my head down and veered quickly into the men's room and locked myself in one of the stalls. I spent the next couple of minutes sitting on the throne, letting the adrenaline rush die down, then unlocked the door and peeked out. The bathroom was empty.

I went to the door and cracked it. I was looking right into the bar, and I scanned the half-dozen patrons occupying its wooden stools. Carlson was at the end, a highball in front of him. He glanced at the front door, drained his glass, ordered another from the bartender. The front door opened and Carlson's head snapped toward it, but he lost interest immediately when a young couple walked in, waved at the bartender, and sat at one of the barrel tables. Carlson was waiting for somebody. I wondered if it could be Leslie.

The door opened again and again Carlson looked up. A tall, slender woman wearing round, Audrey Hepburn dark glasses and a white Valentino suit that must have cost a grand, stopped just inside the doors and looked around the room. She selected a table on the far side of the room and sat down. In spite of the fact that it was considerably darker in the bar than outside, she didn't bother to take off her glasses. She ordered a drink from the cocktail waitress, and Carlson went back to his highball.

I felt like a trapped rat. There was no way I could get out of the restaurant without Carlson burning me. I just hoped he didn't decide to do a repeat of his Code Three bout in here. There were other things I could think to do with my evening than standing in the men's room staring through a crack in the door.

Carlson kept glancing over at the woman in the Valentino suit, who was sipping the martini the waitress had brought her. A sly smile crossed his lips, and he slid off his barstool and carried his drink over to the woman's table.

Carlson said something to her and she looked up. She looked away from him distractedly; then he said something else and she shrugged and he sat down. She picked up her purse from the table, unsnapped it, and took out a cigarette. He lit it with a match and they exchanged a few words. She looked at Carlson and smiled. I took a better look at the woman.

She had dark hair and was maybe in her midforties, but the glasses made it hard to tell. Well preserved, with a lineless, almost gaunt face, but considering the Rodeo Drive ensemble, the three-hundred-dollar hairdo, and the size of the rocks on her hands, plastic surgery was a possibility.

He leaned toward her and said something and laughed. If I hadn't known, I wouldn't have guessed he was a grieving widower, devastated by the death of his wife.

The woman responded to his laughter with a tight smile. Maybe Edith Carlson had been right. Maybe her husband had been chippying around on her, just with a different partner. But somehow I couldn't see it, not with this one. Beverly Hills or Bel Air or wherever she hailed from was a long way from Highland Park. She was probably just down here visiting her fifty-foot yacht and had stopped in for a drink, having no idea she would be pounced upon by an overweight, middle-aged, drunken cop.

She confirmed my appraisal as he kept talking and grinning and her gaze drifted around the bar distractedly, obviously uninterested in whatever he was trying to sell. She exhaled smoke, crushed out the cigarette in the ashtray, and reached into her purse. Carlson pulled his chair closer to her and leaned over further. He slipped his right arm around the back of her chair and hunched over the table, shielding her from view with his back, and whispered something in her ear. His right hand came off the back of the chair and made a furtive move, and although I couldn't be sure, I thought I saw it slip something inside his windbreaker. He leaned back, and she snapped her purse shut and stood up and, without saying another word, walked out of the bar.

I thought about what I had just seen, but not for long. Carlson zipped up his windbreaker and stood and started across the room toward the men's room. I went into the first stall and locked myself in and sat down on the can. I heard the door open and footsteps on the tile floor and then the stall door rattled. The door on the next stall opened and closed, and the lock clicked shut. I heard his windbreaker unzip and then the rustling of paper, like an envelope being opened, and that was all I waited to hear. There was no telling when I would get another chance to get the hell out of there, so I flushed the toilet and opened the stall and made the bathroom door in three giant strides.

I made it out to the parking lot as the woman was pulling out of the lot in a new black Jaguar XJS convertible. I took out the recorder and read off the license: "SHRLYS1."

I trotted to the rental and got in. Five minutes later, Carlson came out of the restaurant and I scrunched down in the seat to keep him from seeing me. He walked back to the pontoon gate, unlocked it, and strode down to the boat. After twenty minutes, he emerged from the boat and came back up the pontoon. Once more, I kept my head low as he got into the Stealth and took off.

He took the Marina freeway back to the San Diego freeway and headed north. Rush-hour traffic thickened to an enervating crawl south of Westwood, and it took us half an hour to make the eight miles over the Sepulveda pass to the valley. Dusk was settling and city lights were twinkling on when he pulled off at the Sepulveda exit and drove to Ventura Boulevard.

He turned right on Ventura and just past Woodman, he suddenly slowed and pulled over to the curb without signaling. I frantically scanned the street for a parking space so that I wouldn't have to drive by him, spotted one half a block down from where he had pulled over, and pulled into it.

A parking valet ran around to Carlson's side of the car and opened the door and Carlson got out. He went into the restaurant and the valet jumped into the Stealth and drove it around the corner. I pulled out and took a look at the place as I cruised by.

It was called La Fleur, one of those small, trendy French restaurants that serve escargots and arugula and goat cheese salad and which you can't get out of for less than forty dollars. Normally I didn't like that sort of place, but this one held a particular charm for me, perhaps because it had big windows that looked out onto the boulevard.

I drove down a block, made a left, and doubled back. My luck was holding. There was an open parking space on the opposite side of the street, directly across from the restaurant. I parked and picked up the binoculars.

The place was not crowded and it was easy to pick out Carlson. He was sitting at a table near the window, talking with a swarthy, jowly man dressed in a brown double-breasted suit. The man ate while he talked; Carlson was occupied with his usual pastime, imbibing. After a couple of minutes, Carlson took a business-size envelope out of his windbreaker and slid it across the table to the man, who picked it up casually and slipped it into his inside breast pocket. After that, Carlson drained his drink and rose. They shook hands and Carlson came outside.

He handed the red-jacketed valet his parking stub, along with a couple of bucks, and the valet sprinted around the corner to fetch his car. Carlson stood, rocking on the balls of his feet, then his eyes drifted across the street and landed on the car, and I ducked my head below the window.

I had no idea if he'd spotted me, or if he recognized the Subaru from the parking lot of Harpoon Harry's, or if he had noticed nothing, but I stayed down until I heard a car door slam and the Stealth take off. I lifted up my head and took a peek. The valet was standing alone in front of the restaurant.

I debated what to do. If Carlson had burned me, nothing I did from now on would make a difference. On the other hand, if he'd recognized the car, or thought he did, he would be watching for a tail. I made up my mind, locked up the car, and ran across the street.

La Fleur smelled of butter and garlic. It seated perhaps sixty, with wood-paneled walls and a six-stool bar, two of which were occupied. I took one of the remaining four, ordered a vodka and soda with lime, and glanced over at the swarthy man.

He had a large head covered with slicked-back black hair, and a very round face that looked as if it would always need a shave. On the table in front of him was a copy of the *Racing Form*.

A Greek-looking waiter came over to the table and said something to the man, who got out a piece of paper, made some notes, and slipped it into his pocket. The waiter drifted away, and I asked the bartender, who was washing glasses, "That man at the table over there—I think I may know him. You know his name?"

The hawk-faced bartender glanced over, went on washing glasses, and said, "Bellasario."

"What's his first name?"

"I wouldn't know."

"He's a steady customer here?"

"He comes in pretty regular, yeah."

I nodded obscurely. "What's his line?"

He looked up from the sink and gave me a cold stare. "I wouldn't know."

I nursed my drink for another fifteen minutes and then Bellasario paid his check and stood up. I let him get outside before I pushed off from the bar and followed.

He was standing on the curb waiting for his car when I came out, and I turned my head away as I walked by him to the curb. I waited for a break in traffic to sprint across the boulevard to my rental. I drove up a block, turned around, and pulled over. While I waited, I did some recording. "At five-forty, subject proceeded to restaurant La Fleur, 35567 Ventura Boulevard, where he met with a man named Bellasario, first name unknown.

The valet brought up a black Lincoln Towncar, and Bellasario tipped him and got in. He headed east on Ventura and I pulled away and trailed behind. A couple of blocks past Coldwater, he signaled and pulled into a parking lot. I gave a quick glance at the free-standing building next to the parking lot as I passed. There was a hot-pink neon martini glass over the door, along with the name: Anthony's. I parked in a space up the block and got my attaché case out of the backseat.

I didn't think that Bellasario had paid any attention to me in Le Fleur, but there was no use taking any chances. I peeled off my jacket, then flipped open the locks on the attaché case and lifted the lid. After surveying the contents, I decided on a canvas hat and pair of thick-rimmed glasses. I put them on and stared at myself in the mirror. Passable. I pocketed the tape recorder and got out of the car.

I located the Towncar in Anthony's parking lot and looked around to make sure I was alone before pulling out the cassette recorder. "Six-ten. Bellasario has gone into Anthony's bar, 11454 Ventura. He's driving a 1991 Lincoln Towncar, California license 659RRT."

I put the recorder in my pants pocket and went around to the front door.

The place was dimly lit, smoky, and noisy, the bar jammed with accomplished drinkers sharing loud and boisterous commentary about the Kings game on the television suspended from the ceiling. Messages were stuck all around the frame of the mirror behind the bar, messages for Al and Jerry and Dave to call home or work or whatever connection they wanted or didn't want to make. I ordered a beer from the fat bartender and scanned the room from under the brim of my hat. Bellasario was on a stool toward the end of the bar. A thick-necked man in a blue sports shirt was standing beside him, talking in his ear, and Bellasario was making notes on a piece of paper. Maybe he was a writer gathering information for a novel, but somehow I doubted it. These people didn't look all that witty that everything they said would be worth taking down. From across the bar, a red-headed man yelled, "Hey, Nick, what's the line on the Rams-Eagles game?"

Bellasario looked up from his notes and shouted back, "Rams by three and a half."

The man waved and turned to discuss the odds with the man on the stool next to him. I left three bucks on the bar and went outside. The night air was like a cool drink of water after the smoky din of the bar. As I walked to the car, I told the recorder that Bellasario's first name was Nick, and that his occupation was probably bookmaker.

Maybe that was how Carlson had managed to pay for a big house on a hill and a thirty-thousand-dollar sports car and a boat in the marina on a cop's salary—betting on football games. Maybe he'd just had a bad day, which would explain the direction that envelope had gone across the table. Maybe the house was mortgaged up to the shingled roof and the car was not his and he'd been working on a friend's boat, making extra money doing repairs. Maybe, but my gut told me otherwise. I just hoped Leslie wasn't part of whatever he was involved in. I liked her. A lot. And I wanted to keep on liking her.

I checked my watch and drove to a phone booth two blocks down and called Greenberg Bail Bonds on the slim chance Rose or Hymie might be working late. Greenberg belonged to Hymie Fein, a once bit-part actor who had grudgingly inherited the business some thirty-five years ago from his mentor, Martin Greenberg, and had not spent a day since not regretting it, in spite of the fact the business had made him rich. Hymie's computer was hooked into all sorts of nifty national data services, and he gave me the use of it at his cost. I, in turn, for expenses only, performed an occasional service for him, like hunt down one of his wards who had decided that a nice trip to New Orleans for a little Cajun cuisine was preferable to dining on prison fare for the next couple of years. A nice I'll-scratch-your-back-you-scratch-mine arrangement that had worked out rather well over the past few years.

I was in luck. Rose Spivak, Hymie's trusted secretary for eleven years, picked up the phone. "Greenberg Bail Bonds. Our bond is our word."

Hymie made her say that every time she answered the phone, and she hated it. "How is the love of my life?"

Her tone turned suspicious. "Who is this?"

"The love of *your* life."

"The love of my life is Big Bob and he doesn't talk. He just hums."

"A new boyfriend?"

"My vibrator."

"At your age?" I chided her. "Rose, you should be ashamed."

"It's because of my age I can't afford to be ashamed. I have to take what I can get. What do you want now, Jake?"

"Information, sweetheart."

"That's all the men I know ever want. That's why I keep Big Bob around."

"You have a pen handy? I have a Christmas list."

"Go ahead."

"I need a credit rundown, property ownership, vehicle and pleasure-craft registrations on an Arthur Carlson, 7766 Owlridge Lane, Highland Park—"

"The property ownership—county or statewide?"

"Statewide. Also, I need registration checks on two California plates, SHRLYS1 and 659RRT."

Her tone turned vexed. It was part of her routine. "You don't want much, do you?"

"I'm not finished yet," I told her.

She sighed. "Of course not."

"Run a criminal conviction record on a Nick Bellasario. B-e-l-l-a-s-a-r-i-o."

I hesitated, then said, "One more thing. Run property and vehicle ownerships for a Leslie Boetticher, residence Manhattan Beach." I spelled out the name for her.

"That's two things," she corrected me. "You want a pleasure-craft registration check on her, too?"

I thought about it. "Might as well."

"When do you need all this?"

"How about tomorrow?"

"Jesus Christ, give me a break. I'd like to get out of here sometime tonight—"

"I wouldn't ask if it wasn't really important, Rose. Pretty pleeeese—"

"Oh, all right," she relented.

"Don't worry," I tried to reassure her, "Big Bob will be waiting for you when you get home."

"That's the one good thing about him," she agreed. "He never goes out on me."

Twenty-six

I got home at quarter after seven, stuck a frozen fettuccine Alfredo in the microwave, and checked my messages. Another call from Leslie, this time with her home number. I started to dial it, then hesitated. I found myself thinking about her all the time, remembering the time we'd spent together and fantasizing about times we hadn't yet. I felt as if I could get sucked in over my head with her, and that would not be the smartest thing in the world I could do, at least not until I got that information back from Rose tomorrow. On the other hand, I didn't want her to think I was avoiding her. After all, it was only a phone call.

She answered on the second ring. "Hello."

"Leslie. Jake."

"The missing man. Where are you?"

"Home. I just got in."

"Have you eaten?"

I glanced at the microwave. "Not yet."

"I'm cooking lasagna if you'd like to drop by."

"Your place?"

"That's where I normally cook," she said. "My place."

I thought about lasagna. I thought about her legs. I thought

167

about her legs wrapped around my back. To hell with being smart. "It'll take me about half an hour, depending on traffic."

"I'll put the lasagna in the oven now," she said, and gave me directions.

I stopped at a liquor store and picked up two bottles of chardonnay and hit the freeway. Traffic was light and I made it to Manhattan Beach in twenty-five minutes. It was a sleepy little beach town of trendy, semiquaint brick and wood-shingle shops, the lights from which shone gauzily through the thick fog that had rolled in from the ocean. I had to stop repeatedly and get out of the car to make out the names on the street signs through the gray soup, but finally managed to locate the address, a small, two-story duplex two blocks from the beach.

Spaces on the street were slim, and I was forced to park three blocks away and walk back. By the time I trudged up the outside stairs and knocked on her door, I was shivering from the wet mist that had penetrated my clothes.

The chill was momentarily forgotten when she opened the door. Her hair was up and she had on a blue turtleneck sweater and a pair of tight jeans. We gave each other a greeting kiss and I stepped inside and she closed the door.

"Nice weather out there."

She nodded. "It rolled in about an hour ago. I like the fog, though. Makes me feel cozy to be inside."

I handed her the wine and she looked in the bag. "You didn't have to do that."

"I didn't? Hell, then I'll return it and get my money back."

Her eyes crinkled when she smiled. "Like hell you will. Sit by the fire and get warm and I'll pour us a couple of glasses. Unless you want a cocktail?"

"No, wine is fine."

She went into the kitchen and I looked around. The living room was small, warm, and intimate. The furniture was modern, but not particularly expensive, a green velveteen couch and matching armchairs, glass coffee and end tables, lamps of fake brass, a color TV and stereo system on a rolling cart. The round glass-top dining table in the small alcove by the kitchen was set for two, complete with candles in silver holders. I thought about the cold fog outside and started to feel cozy, too.

I drifted over to the four well-stocked bookshelves set into the wall and scanned the titles. They ran about fifty-fifty between nonfiction volumes of criminology and true crime and good fiction by writers like Hemingway, Shaw, Jones, Styron. I liked her taste. Next to the bookshelves, a fake log burned in the gas fireplace. I stood in front of it and warmed my hands and looked at the framed photographs that lined the mantel. Most of them were of Leslie in the company of assorted, rugged-looking Tom Selleck types, on boats, at the beach, skiing. In one, she was dressed in her LAPD blues and Sam Browne belt, standing in front of a black-and-white with a young, handsome patrolman.

"My first patrol car," her voice said behind me.

I turned around and she handed me a glass of wine. "Was that your partner? The one who was killed?"

She nodded solemnly. "Yeah. That was Fred."

I picked up the picture next to it and looked at it. Leslie looked much younger, her smile radiating exuberance and innocence. She stood in front of a small cottage, flanked by an older couple. The man was big shouldered and big bellied, like a football player gone to seed. The gray-haired woman was small and frail looking and had Leslie's eyes.

"My parents," she said, a bit wistfully. "That was taken right before dad died, eight years ago."

"He looked like a young man in that picture."

She nodded. "Forty-four. His heart just stopped one day at work and he keeled over, dead. When my mother called me and told me, I couldn't believe it."

"You were close?"

"Yeah, we were."

The woman had seen a lot of death in her short life. I felt guilty for dredging it up. "Your mother still alive?"

"Uh-huh." She smiled enigmatically. "We're not so close."

"Why not?"

She shrugged. "My mother is a deeply religious woman who likes to deliver long sermons about the Seven Deadly Sins. The two she usually chooses to preach to me about are vanity and avarice, which she thinks I've cornered the market on. She always used to accuse me of having delusions of grandeur, of thinking I was better than everybody else. Except her idea of 'everybody else' is everybody else living in squalor in Youngstown. Her idea of what I should have done with my life is marry some local steelworker with grime on his neck and settle down and raise a brood of brats in a grimy little cottage like the one she's lived in for the past thirty years. She just can't understand how I would want a life better than she and my father had. You think there's something wrong with wanting more?"

"Nothing that I can see."

"I don't, either. It's the American dream, it's what this country is based on. But it's not my mother's dream. Somehow, she sees my moving out as some sort of personal attack on her life-style and the City of God. I send her money every month to help her out—Dad didn't leave much behind—but she even resents that. Keeps saying she doesn't need my charity. Every time I call, it always seems to wind up in the same old argument. Consequently, I don't call much."

"Families are wonderful."

She smiled. "You have any?"

"I'm lucky. Everyone's dead."

"No brothers or sisters?"

"Nope. Only child."

"Well, only child, I hope you're hungry. Dinner should be ready in ten minutes."

"I am." I waved my wineglass at the room. "I like your place."

"Thanks. The rent is too high—a thousand a month—but that's the beach. I've often thought of being practical and moving somewhere inland to save the money, but I can't bring myself to do it. Besides, I don't spend money on much else, so what the hell, I guess I'm entitled to live where I want."

"How much does a homicide detective make these days?"

"Fifty-six five. But the overtime can add a little on to that."

Fifty-six five. Plenty for a single girl to live on, but not a hell of a lot for a married man with a mortgage and a boat and a new car. Leslie moved over to the couch and sat down. "I tried to reach you all day today. You were out."

"I picked up a couple of cases from two attorneys I know," I hedged.

She lifted a curious eyebrow. "You're dropping the Graves matter?"

I shrugged. "There's nothing left to carry. It's Schayes' and Grabner's case and they seemed satisfied that Gilman did the deed."

She sipped her wine. "But are you?"

"Yeah," I lied. "I am. Anyway, I can't continue to ignore my paying clients. I don't have that many of them."

She nodded as if she found that decision wise.

"How was Sheena's day in the jungle?" I asked, trying to divert her inquiries.

"The animals were restless," she said. "A man stabbed his wife of ten years to death after she complained that he'd put a tire iron in the trunk of her car, causing it to rattle around and bother her. Then two guys beat a friend of theirs sense-less and dropped a twenty-pound block of cement on his head over an argument as to who was the best rap singer. Just a typical day in the life of a homicide detective."

I shook my head. "I don't know how you do it."

She blinked. "What?"

"Cope."

She thought about it and shrugged. "I probably wouldn't be able to if I stopped and thought about what it means. But you can't. You can't take the time to ponder philosophical questions about good and evil and the nature of man. You look at a body and it's a piece of a puzzle, that's all. You don't think about who that person was or what he died for. You look at the direction of the blood spatters, whether a bullet hole is an entry or exit wound, whether the body shows signs of rigor. You can't let the absurdity of it touch you or it'll overwhelm you and you'll drown. Even the horror leaves after a while. You start to doubt your own ability to feel anything. That's what you have to watch, that it doesn't spill over into your normal, non-cop life." She looked at her watch. "I'd better start tossing the salad, unless you want burned lasagna."

"Can I help?"

"You can light the candles and turn on some music. Matches are in the ashtray on the coffee table."

"Consider it done."

She went into the kitchen and I performed my assigned duties with precision, locating some Jobim on the stereo dial and dimming the lights to add a more romantic atmosphere. She came out with the lasagna, salad, and garlic toast, then went back for more wine.

The garlic toast was crisp and delicious and the vinaigrette she had tossed the salad with was excellent, but the topper was the lasagna. I was impressed and I told her so, enthusiastically.

"Actually, I love to cook." she said, forking a mouthful of pasta into her mouth. "That's one thing I got from my mother. I don't do it too much because I have nobody to cook for."

"Doesn't Carlson ever come over for dinner?" I fished.

She shook her head. "That would have only been adding fuel to the fire that was stoking his wife. I've avoided socializing with Art after office hours for that very reason."

I finished the last bite of lasagna and filled our wineglasses. "How is Carlson doing, by the way?" I asked, trying to sound casual.

Her tone became subdued. "All right."

"You talk to him today?"

She put her fork down as if she had suddenly lost her appetite and pushed her plate away. "This morning."

"What'd he have to say?"

She hesitated. Her eyes were troubled. "I'm worried about him."

"Why? What's the matter?"

"This can't go past this table."

"No problem."

"When I called him, he was already half-smashed and it was only nine in the morning. He made some strange, half-rambling remarks that didn't make any sense. It was the tone of his voice that really got me. He sounded, I don't know, different. Not like himself at all. I got worried and asked him if he was OK, did he want me to come over there, and he said, no, he was fine. He had to go out and collect a debt to pay off a debt. I asked him what debt, and he got evasive, said it was just personal stuff."

"Is he in hock to somebody?"

"I don't know," she said, chewing her food thoughtfully. "To tell you the truth, lately, I don't know much about Art's life. He's changed over the past year, become almost like a stranger. He used to tell me everything that was going on in his life, but lately, he's just sort of withdrawn into himself. And the drinking has really gotten a lot worse. He's started to drink on the job. I've had to cover for him more than a couple of times. He'll disappear on me for hours, then show up smashed. I've told him it's got to stop, that it isn't just his career he's jeopardizing, it's mine, too."

"What does he say?"

"Oh, he's very contrite. Apologizes and says it won't happen again. Maybe he even means it at the time, but I know he's just bullshitting himself and me. I've tried to talk him into getting some help, but he says he's in control of the situation, that he doesn't need any help." She shook her head. "Enough about Art."

She got up, picked up the plates, and carried them into the

kitchen. We sat on the couch, drinking wine, and she snuggled against me. "I've been thinking about last night all day," she said softly.

"So have I."

"I've been thinking about an encore."

"I haven't."

She sat upright and looked at me, her eyes hurt. "No?"

"No. I've been thinking about a new show. One with a few more acts."

She smiled. "I like that idea."

She took my hand and led me into the small bedroom. I undressed and got under the quilted covers while she lighted candles all over the room. By the time she'd finished, the place looked like a shrine in St. Patrick's.

I watched her as she undressed, captivated by the elegant lines of her body bathed in the glow of the candles, and then she slipped into bed and we were all hands and legs and mouths. She told me to talk dirty to her and I did and she became frantic, bucking and thrashing, digging her nails into my buttocks, pulling me into her, slamming me into her, harder and harder, until we both came in convulsive explosions of ecstasy.

Afterward, we lay there, sweating and spent, and she said, "That was incredible. Better than last night." She paused. "I'd forgotten how great sex could be. You're the first man I've been with in over a year, ever since I broke up with my boyfriend."

"That's a long time."

"It's funny. The less you have it, the less you want it." She stroked my crotch. "You've started something now. I'm going to be wanting it all the time. So you'd better be prepared."

"I'll do my best, ma'am." Outside the window, the surf hissed rhythmically against the shore. "You know you said Carlson has been disappearing on you lately?"

Her body stiffened slightly. "Yeah?"

I thought about how to frame the question. I couldn't come up with a way that didn't sound like the question itself, so I just asked it: "How about the day his wife died?"

She lifted her head off my chest and stared into my eyes. "Why do you ask that?"

"No particular reason."

She wasn't buying that, not that I expected her to. "Oh, no you don't. There *is* a reason and I want to know what it is."

"There is no reason. Really."

We both knew I was lying. We also both knew I was not going to tell the truth tonight. She looked at me and said, her voice flat: "We were together all day."

She got out of bed and slipped into a robe, then left the room. I could hear her moving around in the kitchen, turning on the tap, and I lay there, mentally kicking myself in the ass. My timing, as usual, was impeccable.

She returned momentarily and stood in the doorway, her arms folded across her chest. "It's too bad you don't trust me enough to be honest with me."

"It's not that—"

"I'm kind of tired and I have an early day tomorrow," she said.

Not one to miss an exit cue, I got out of bed and dressed. She showed me to the door and pecked me with a perfunctory good-night kiss.

I pinched my jacket closed to keep out the dampness and walked to my car, wondering about her reaction to my question about Carlson. Something bothered her about it, more than my asking it or refusing to reveal my reasons for asking it. Something about the question itself. My ruminations were cut short as I opened my car door and was startled by the dark shape that materialized like a wraith out of the fog. Instinctively, I cocked my right fist back, but the shape stopped on the other side of the car door and said menacingly, "Stay away from her."

It was Carlson and he was plastered. "Carlson. What are you doing here?"

"Just keep away from her. She's my girl."

"Maybe you should talk that over with her."

"I don't need to talk it over with her," he growled. "I'm talking it over with you. Keep away from her."

I closed the door just in case he decided to slam it shut on me and stepped away from the car, ready for him to make a move. I would take no pleasure in beating up a man in his condition, no matter how little I liked him, but I didn't intend to stand there and get punched in the face, either. "You're drunk," I said. "Go home."

"I'm warning you, Asch. My life is a runaway. I've gone too far to go back. She made sure of that. She put me on the goddamn train, just like she put Hodges on, only I ain't getting off the way he did. So we're both on, and that's it. There ain't any room for any more passengers, so don't try to get on board. You understand?"

I didn't understand. I wasn't even sure if the "she" he was talking about was his dead wife or Leslie. The man was wound up and unpredictable and I didn't want to provoke him, but he was starting to piss me off. "I don't have the slightest idea what you're talking about, Carlson. What train? Who the hell is Hodges?"

He took a lurching step forward, his fists balled at his sides, and I shifted my weight, getting ready to take him out. "Just stay away from her," he snarled, the threat thick in his voice. "I'm warning you. I'll make a fucking ashtray out of you."

As suddenly as he had appeared, he was gone. I stood, listening to his footsteps retreating in the fog, feeling as if I had just entered the Twilight Zone. The man definitely had problems, what kind I was not sure. He *was* violent, of that I *was* sure, and a violent man with problems was a dangerous man, especially if he carried a gun.

I considered returning to Leslie's apartment and relating the incident, but decided against it, at least until I got a look at those reports tomorrow.

I drove home and got into bed and rode on a train all night long. I was the only one in the coach car and there was no conductor, but it didn't need any because it never stopped anywhere, it just rolled along, its wheels clacking on the track, blowing its shrill whistle into blackness.

Twenty-seven

The next morning, I returned the rental and retrieved my own car. Since I was on the meter, I decided I'd better go to work, so I drove over to Larrabee's Chevrolet on Figueroa and talked with Philip Brodsky, who turned out to be an overweight, sandy-haired man with an affable manner and a wide smile.

Over coffee, Brodsky protested his innocence, saying the cops had unfairly rigged the identification process, putting him in a lineup with five men who looked nothing like him. The frock in his closet, he explained, was not a *doctor's* frock, but an *artist's* frock Brodsky wore when he painted. (The cops *did* find oil paints and an easel in the apartment). As for the list of names, it was a list of prospective clients he had pulled out of the credit applications at the dealership. After all, he was a car salesman, and he wanted to sell cars. He had pulled out all immigrant names because he thought they would be "easier pickings," and that he could sell them more options they didn't need, and therefore make more money. Perhaps not very ethical, but certainly not against the law. His previous conviction had been for selling worthless desert land to gullible buyers in Arizona. Again Brodsky claimed he was an innocent dupe, that he had just been a salesman for the phony land development company, and that he'd been taken in just like the poor suckers to whom he'd sold subdivided sand.

His story was total bullshit, of course. The man was guilty as hell. All I could do was interview the four women, try to convince them that they would be humiliated by a court trial, and that recounting their stories on the stand was only going to cause them embarrassment when the media blasted their names and faces all over the television screen. If that failed, Resnick's only hope, outside of a plea bargain, would be that no jury would believe that anybody could be so stupid as to pay some stranger hundreds of dollars to dip his wick. I did have to hand it to the guy—he had balls, a fact to which at least four women could attest.

After interviewing Brodsky, I drove out to the address I had for Maria Elizondo, the woman who had brought the original complaint against Philip Brodsky. The apartment was in the projects in a rundown building covered with *placa*. Half a dozen gangbangers hung around out front, watching me with black, suspicious eyes as I got out of my car, and I felt uneasy under their alien gaze. I felt even un-easier when the door of the apartment was answered by a big Mexican man in a stained summer undershirt and gang tat-toos all over his arms.

The man did not speak much English, but I spoke enough Spanish to determine that he was Maria's boyfriend, that she worked as a maid days and would not be back until later that night. Determining that telling him who I was and what I wanted might not be the wisest course of action, I told him simply that I was "an investigator looking into her case," and that I would get in touch with her some other time.

The punks were still hanging around out front when I came out, and I was pleasantly surprised to find that my car was not on blocks. Not even a key mark on the paint. I got in the car and surveyed the street. This was going to be a tough one. I clearly didn't want to interview Maria in the presence of her boyfriend, which meant I was going to have to find out where she worked. The simplest way would be to stake out the place and follow her, but this wouldn't be the easiest or safest neighborhood to set up a surveillance. Anyway, I didn't even know what the woman looked like. I'd have to go through the credit application Maria had made out at Larrabee's Chevrolet and see if it listed a current employer or a credit reference.

The rest of the morning and part of the afternoon was spent at Westside, trying to track down the names of staff that happened to be on duty the night Amos Welk had his butt set ablaze. The doctor who had performed the surgery refused to talk to me, and after going through several uncooperative, tight-lipped administrators, I called Schindler and told him there would be little I could do until he subpoenaed the hospital's employment records.

It was a little after two when I walked through the hallowed portals of Greenberg Bail Bonds. Rose stopped typing and peered at me over the tops of her horn-rimmed glasses. "I was wondering when you were going to get here."

She was wearing a loose-fitting muu-muu with flowers all over it, and she'd dyed her hair since I'd last seen her two weeks ago, something she did as often as some people changed their underwear. This time it was fire engine red.

I placed two bottles of Chivas—twice the customary tribute—on her desk. "For heroic performance above the call of duty. By the way, you look absolutely ravishing today, my dear."

She eyed the two bottles, then me, and said sourly, "Thanks. You look as full of shit as you are."

"You missed your calling, Rose. You should have been a hostess in Washington. They could have used someone with your diplomatic charm. I love your hair, by the way."

She grunted disbelievingly, sat down at her desk and put the scotch away in a drawer. She waved a hand at the computer, which was busy printing out and said, "Your credit and property checks are in. The DMV stuff is coming in now."

Through the open inner-office door, Hymie's voice raised in pitch, indicating that he was speaking to one of his customers. "You're a peach, Rose," I said appreciatively. "I'll just go say hello to Hymie."

Hymie was at his desk, talking on the phone. He was dressed like a golfer from Iowa, in a lime-green suit, yellow shirt, yellow and green paisley tie, and white belt. He ran a hand over his white hair and said, "Sorry, no collateral, no bond, Jesse. You know the rules. I don't care if you got no priors. Go ahead and wait and see if you can get out on OR. The report will take seventy-two hours to work up. You want to stay in for seventy-two hours, see if that's the recommendation, fine with me."

He waved me into a chair, made a face, and went on: "You got a house? How about a car? What kind? How much you owe on it?" He listened, shook his head. "Too much. You got *anything?* Jewelry? A motorcycle? How about your relatives? Can they raise fifteen hundred?"

I'd sat here listening to this drama a hundred times before. Hymie had listened to it ten thousand. His eyes rolled up impatiently. "Look, you call your people. You raise the fifteen hundred, OK. Otherwise, you're in until the trial. Call me back."

He hung up and twirled his white mustache between two fingers. "These people are fucking amazing, Jake. Just fucking amazing. They think I'm in this business as some sort of charity gig, Help the Stupid, or something. Here's a jerk—a Mexican gardener—works for some rich couple in Westlake. They're on vacation in Europe and they come home a couple of days early and walk into their house and find big plastic trash bags sitting on the living room floor. The husband looks in them and finds they're full of the household silver and everything else that isn't tied down.

"About that time, a guy with a stocking mask on comes walking out of the bedroom carrying another bag. He's also wearing a khaki outfit like their gardener Jesse wears, and it's got an embroidered name tag on the pocket that says 'Jesse.' Well, as soon as old Jesse sees his employers standing in the middle of the room, staring at him with their mouths open, he drops the fucking bag and books through the back door. The owner of the house starts chasing him, yelling, 'Jesse, why are you stealing from us?' You know what Jesse yells back?"

I told him I was afraid to guess.

"'It ain't me!'"

I had to laugh.

"Now this brain-dead asshole calls me to tell me he can only raise eight hundred of the fifteen hundred he needs for the bond and wants me to give him the other seven on credit." He shook his head again. "The people you gotta deal with in this business. Garbage. I'm telling you, Jake, it's the shittiest business in the world. You live in jails, everybody hates you. Clerks, crooks, cops." He jabbed a thumb at the phone and said angrily, "This jerk thinks I'm trying to rip him off. He thinks I'm a thief. A piece of crud who tries to steal from the people who pay him, and he thinks I'm a thief."

The lament was one I heard every time I came into the office. A lot of people in this world didn't particularly like what they did for a living. They did it because they had a skill and had to live and did not know what else they would do if they had the chance. I knew. I was one of those people. Hymie's distaste for the bail-bond business, however, was a subject he never tired of vocalizing. In fact, he rarely talked about anything else. When he *did* talk about something else, it was inevitably about some get-rich scheme he had that would take him *out* of the bail-bond business. The last one had been hospital gowns with Velcro in the back so that your cheeks would not be exposed while you shuffled down the hall to X ray.

I'd politely declined a partnership in that capitalistic endeavor, as I had every other investment opportunity Hymie had offered me. I also would be declining the latest, which, by the sudden electrified look in his eyes I knew he would be explaining to me shortly.

He stood up from his desk and took off his jacket, and said, "Sit right there. I'll be right back."

He went into the other room and a few minutes later came

back dressed in an orange jumpsuit, the kind the prisoners at the county jail wore as they were paraded, manacled, into court.

"You know what this is?" he said, closing the door.

"An improvement over your usual ensemble."

He frowned. "Very funny. *This*"——he said, pausing significantly—"is private jets, mansions in Bel Air, yachts in the Mediterranean. Behold."

He hit the light switch, plunging the room into darkness. All I could see was the jumpsuit, glowing with an eerie fluorescent orange light. Hymie's disembodied voice floated out of the darkness: "Well?"

"Don't tell me. You're making your motion-picture comeback as Claude Rains'offspring in *Son of the Invisible Man*."

The lights went back on and he stared at me with a chagrined look. "Don't be ridiculous."

"You're doing weekends in the county jail and you're out on furlough," I guessed. "I didn't know they let you take the suits home. What'd they get you for?"

"You didn't *see* it?"

"See what?"

"The *suit*."

"I saw it. What about it?"

He nodded and his expression turned serious, the same expression he always assumed when he started to go into his pitch. "You know how many prisoners there are in county jails across the country?"

"Can't say that I do. How many?"

His brow furrowed and he frowned. "I don't know. But there have to be thousands. Millions, maybe."

"I'll take your word for it."

"If you were a prisoner and you were going to try to escape, when would you do it?"

I shrugged. "On Columbus Day."

He made a face. "I'm serious. When would you try to escape—in the daytime when you could be seen, or at night when it's dark and your chances of getting away were much better?"

I saw where he was heading, but there was no way to stop him, so I went along. "At night."

"Exactly!" he said, pleased. "I was sitting in court one day, watching the prisoners shuffle in, and the thought just struck me like a bolt of lightning. If the jumpsuits could be seen in the dark, the cops would have a much easier time spotting escaping prisoners and hunting them down. So I got one and had it dipped in luminous paint. It only costs a few bucks. Every jail in the country will buy them. We'll clean up."

His use of the plural pronoun made me slightly uneasy, but I said nothing.

"I've worked out all the figures," he assured me. "We can start out with a thousand. That'll get the unit cost down to about thirty bucks. Advertising, promotion, another ten thousand. For twenty thousand, you can be a fifty-fifty partner."

I tried to put a lot of regret in my voice. "My cash flow is a little light this month, Hymie. Maybe you'd better look for another partner."

"You gotta take risks in this world if you expect to get anywhere," he admonished me.

"I know. And it really pains me to turn down the opportunity. The idea is a natural. But I just can't swing that kind of cash right now."

Thankfully, his phone rang again and he went back to his desk and picked it up. "Huh? Who is this? Oh, yeah, Frank. What'd you do this time? OK. Give yourself up and call me. OK, then come in this afternoon and I'll take you over."

I took the opportunity to escape and waved good-bye.

Rose handed me a stack of reports and said, "That'll be a hundred and thirty dollars."

I wrote her out a check and asked if I could use the phone. She pointed at the one on the other desk. "Use line two."

The service had another message from Leslie and one from Glenn, telling me to call him at his office, that the toxicology report had come in.

"Chloral hydrate and alcohol," he said.

"The old Mickey Finn."

"Yep."

"What kind of levels?"

"Blood alcohol was point one five, chloral hydrate three point zero percent."

"Would that be enough to put someone to sleep?"

"Depends on the person's tolerance level. Her tolerance level must have been pretty high, according to what her husband and the doctor say. That bottle had fifty pills in it two weeks ago. There were only half a dozen left."

"They find any capsule residue in her stomach?"

"Just a sec." There was a rustling of papers as he looked through the report. "It's not mentioned here."

"That means they didn't find any?"

"The pathologist is a good one. I'm sure he would've noted it if he had."

"Isn't that kind of strange that she would take pills and there wouldn't be any residue?"

"Not necessarily. Depends on how long before she died she took the pills. A lot of times with pill addicts, you don't find any residue. The stomach gets used to the drug and dumps it immediately into the intestinal tract."

"Did they do a tox on the stomach contents?"

"No. Just blood and liver."

"Why not?"

"Because there was no need. She died of a gunshot wound." There was a pause. "What are you trying to say, that the woman was drugged and murdered?"

"It's possible, isn't it?"

"Anything is possible. But who would go to all that trouble?"

"Anybody who wanted to make it look like suicide."

"The only one with a possible motive was her husband and he worked all day."

"You're probably right," I said. "Look, thanks, Glenn."

"No problem. Let's get together and tipple a few soon."

"You got it."

My mind was troubled as I hung up. When I looked over the reports that Rose had given me, it was even more troubled.

The Dodge Stealth and the boat in the marina were both registered in Arthur Carlson's name. The boat was an '86 Silverton cruiser he had purchased a year and a half ago from Bremer Yacht Sales for $56,500, with $11,300 down and payments of $466.91 per month for 240 months. Five months ago, he had paid off the balance. The Stealth did not appear on his TRW, which meant he had paid cash for it, somewhere in the neighborhood of thirty grand. He showed a real estate balance—his home, probably—of $68,050, on a loan taken out three years ago with Security Pacific Bank for $196,000. His monthly payments were $956 a month, indicating he had been paying off the principal in sizable chunks. Over the past three years, Carlson had shelled out a minimum of $290,000, which added up to a lot of winners at the track. Too damned many. If there had been any doubt in my mind before, there wasn't any longer. Arthur Carlson was a dirty cop.

The owner of the Lincoln Towncar came up NB Enterprises, with a Ventura Boulevard address. My suspicions about Bellasario were confirmed when I saw that he had two convictions for bookmaking. Leslie said Carlson told her he'd collected a debt to pay a debt. The owner of the Jag, from whom he'd collected, was listed as Shirley Melnick, 822 Whittier Drive, Beverly Hills. Was Carlson acting as a runner for Bellasario, collecting money from his Beverly Hills patrons? Somehow, I couldn't picture the woman driving the Jag placing a hundred-dollar bet on the Rams. But then I couldn't picture *anybody* placing a hundred-dollar bet on the Rams.

Melnick. Melnick. The name rang a bell, but the bell was stuffed with cotton. I tried to remember where I'd heard it, but it kept eluding me, staying just out of my grasp.

I picked up Leslie Boetticher's credit report with trepidation, not really wanting to look at it, dreading what I would find. My dread turned to profound relief when I found that it looked like my own. In 1988, she had purchased a Ford Bronco for fourteen grand and had paid it off in 1991, but that was the only vehicle she owned. She owned no boats and no property in the state, and her TRW showed several late payments on credit card statements. There were two recent inquiries, from Smith Brothers Financial and Bank of America, indicating that she had applied for loans.

I picked up the phone and Rose said testily, "We *are* trying to run a business here."

"I'll be off in a second," I assured her, and dialed the number of the *Chronicle*. The receptionist transferred me to the library, and I asked the clerk to look up what they had in their files on Shirley Melnick. After putting me on hold for a few minutes, she came back on the line and said there were two articles, one from two weeks ago and the other from last Wednesday. "You want me to read the headings?" she asked.

"Please."

"The one two weeks ago is titled 'Millionaire Businessman Disappears Mysteriously.' The other one is 'Police Fear Foul Play in Businessman's Disappearance.'"

I remembered the case. Melnick, a wealthy clothing manufacturer, had disappeared after leaving his downtown plant one night. I'd seen the wife interviewed tearfully on the news, saying she feared that something terrible had happened to her husband. I wondered if her eyes were still red and puffy behind her dark glasses.

I asked the librarian if I could get copies of the articles, and she told me I could pick them up at the front desk in half an hour. I was about to hang up when, on a whim, I asked her to run Leslie Boetticher's name through the computer. It came up three times. I asked the woman to run them off for me, too, then hung up and blew Rose a kiss. "Thanks for everything, sweetie. You have a nice evening home tonight with that Chivas and Bob."

"That's another good thing about Bob," she said. "He doesn't drink."

"Just make sure you don't spill any and short him out."

"That would be a tragedy," she said.

Twenty-eight

The articles were in an envelope at the *Chronicle*'s reception desk when I got there, and I took it next door to Sam's Deli and read them over a cold beer and rare roast beef on rye, starting with the Melnick disappearance.

According to the first article, Melnick—owner of Alida's Fashions, a company that manufactured top-line women's wear—was reported missing on November 28, when he failed to come home from work. Police found his car, a 1992 Mercedes sedan, in an alley four blocks away. The last person to see Melnick was a security guard at the Alida plant on Seventh Street, who had said good night to Melnick as the latter had left at nine-thirty. Melnick had been working late on a new summer line of fashions. "I'm going out of my mind with worry," Melnick's wife, Shirley, was quoted as saying. "I know something has happened to Gary. He wouldn't just leave his car like that and walk away." The investigator on the case, LAPD Detective Ron McCrary, told the reporter that there did not seem to be any motive for the disappearance and that "foul play was suspected."

The second article was more or less just a follow-up of the

first, saying that Melnick was still missing, and that certain physical evidence obtained from the Mercedes indicated that the businessman had indeed been abducted.

One of the articles was about the jewelry store shootout, "Female Officer Downs Killer in Blazing Gun Battle." The events were pretty much as Leslie had recounted them at the Code Three.

The man she had killed, Leonard Dotson, was a convicted felon with a long list of arrests for burglary, assault, and armed robbery. At the time of the shootout, in fact, he had been out on bail on an aggravated assault beef. Evidence found in his apartment indicated that he had been the burglar responsible for seven jewelry store burglaries in the Hollywood area over the past ten months. Leslie's partner, Fred Hodges, had died instantly from taking two bullets in the face. He was survived by his widow, Annette, and his daughter, Trisha.

Fred Hodges. The Hodges Carlson had been babbling about last night.

The other two articles were a short piece about Leslie's decoration for bravery stemming from the shootout, and another about her subsequent promotion to detective.

I put the articles back into the envelope, paid the check, then used the pay phone in the men's room to call Jim Gordon. "Jim, do you know an LAPD detective named Ron McCrary?"

"Yeah, I know McCrary. Why?"

"I need to know the status of one of his cases. He isn't likely to talk to me, but he'd probably tell you."

"What case?"

"The Gary Melnick disappearance."

"The *shmatte* mogul."

"Right."

"What do you need to know?"

"What's going on with the investigation, if they have any theories—"

"He's going to want to know why I'm asking. You know something?"

"I wish I did. His name came up in another investigation. I'm trying to figure out the connection."

"Call me back in ten minutes."

When I did, he told me: "Looks like Melnick was snatched. They found some blood on the front seat of his car. Not a lot, but it was Melnick's type. They think somebody was waiting for him in the parking lot of Alida's, got into his car with him, had him drive to an alley, where he was put into another car."

"Kidnapping?"

"They thought so at first, but when no ransom demand came, they shitcanned that idea."

"Robbery?"

"Possible. Apparently he usually carried a pretty good roll on him. McCrary's also looking at the wife. Hard."

"Looking at her how?"

"The word is that the Melnicks weren't the loviest couple in the world. They'd been married for six years, and the last two were pretty sour. Before he dropped out of sight, Melnick told some friends that he intended to divorce her. Apparently, that didn't sit too well with her. The business belonged to Gary Melnick before they'd married, and she had signed a prenuptial agreement. A divorce would have left her out in the cold, but with him gone, she still has access to the bank accounts. If he's declared legally dead, she inherits."

"Where was she the night he disappeared?"

"At some hotsy-totsy social party. Lots of witnesses."

"They think she hired somebody?"

"It's a possibility they're looking into, that's all I can tell you. You know how investigations like this go. You just throw a lot of shit on the wall and hope some of it sticks." He paused. "If you do come up with something—"

"Of course," I said. "Thanks again, Jim."

Twenty-nine

A typist friend of mine at LAPD's Metro Division gave me the rundown on the two officers who had popped Graves for possession of burglar's tools. Waverly Barker was still with the PD and worked the night shift, but his ex-partner, James Hill, had retired on a disability seven months ago. With a little coaxing, she gave me Hill's phone number and address in Alhambra.

The house was a small white stucco affair with a red-trimmed roof and a patch of browning lawn out front, just like all the other water-rationed lawns on the block. Mother Nature's subtle reminder to Southern California dwellers that in spite of appearances, they still lived in a desert.

I knocked on the door and waited. A set of wind chimes jangled in the breeze at the corner of the house. I was about to knock again when the door was opened by a paunchy middle-aged man dressed in a blue sweatsuit. His gray, jowly face was fixed in a sour expression, as if he was just waiting for me to break out the *Watchtower* so he could boot my ass into the street.

"Yeah?"

"Mr. Hill?"

"Yeah?"

I took out my wallet and gave him a card. "My name is Asch, Mr. Hill. I'm a private investigator. I'm working on a case that involves an arrest you made a couple of years ago, and I was wondering if I could talk to you about it."

He was still suspicious, but he seemed to relax a little, once he learned that I wasn't going to try to talk him into bribing God to let him into heaven by buying his latest primer. "What arrest?"

"William Alan Graves."

He thought back. "Graves. . . ."

"May I come in? I won't take up much of your time—"

He shrugged. "Hell, that's all I got these days."

He pulled open the door and I stepped inside. The living room was done in cheap Early American liberally draped with lace doilies. Hill closed the door and limped over to a green velveteen easy chair in front of the brick fireplace. He winced as he sank into the chair and said, "Got to keep off my feet as much as possible. Bad back."

I sat on the couch. On the television, a woman was trying to guess the price of a stereo system, a new Hyundai, and a washer-dryer combination on "The Price is Right." I said, "Nice place."

He made a face. "My wife's taste. Personally I hate lace, but what the hell, you gotta put up with some things, right? She puts up with enough crap from me." He looked at my card again and said, "Private investigator, huh? I was thinking about getting into that when my back gets better, just for something to do. I got three-quarters of my pension and disability, but I'm going buggy sitting around the house. The wife works all day."

"What happened to your back?"

"Screwed it up chasing some fifteen-year-old glue-sniffer over a wall. A man my age has no business chasing fifteen-year-olds over walls. I'll bet you don't have to do much of that in your line of work."

I had to admit that was true.

He nodded. "What kind of stuff do you do?"

"Depends. Legal stuff, mostly. Trial preparation. Civil, criminal."

"That might be the ticket," he said, shifting in his chair. "Better than working as a security guard in a mall somewhere. My luck, I'd end up chasing some fifteen-year-old shoplifter over a wall and wind up a paraplegic."

"When you get ready to work," I said, "give me a call. We'll talk about it."

His gray face brightened. "Gee, thanks. Maybe I'll do that. Now what about this Graves guy?"

I refreshed his memory about the details of the arrest. If his back was bad, there was nothing wrong with his mind. "I remember the little puke now. Whaddya want to know?"

"I looked over your arrest report. The bust looked pretty good on paper."

"Oh, yeah," he said with a wave of his hand. "We had the fucker dead-bang."

"Then why did he walk?"

"I went to the prosecutor and asked him to drop it."

"Why?"

"Because I was asked to."

"By whom?"

His look turned cagey again. "What's your interest in Graves? You working for a lawyer defending him or something?"

I shook my head. "Graves is dead. He was murdered last week."

"No shit. I didn't hear about it." He lifted an eyebrow. "I can't say I'm surprised. Guys like that usually wind up dead sooner or later."

"Guys like what? Snitches?"

He nodded. "You still didn't say what your interest is."

I explained the situation and he listened thoughtfully. "You figure Graves snitched somebody off and got wasted for it?"

"It's a thought," I said. "Who asked you to go to the DA?"

"A homicide detective from the Hollywood Division," he said. "Carlson. Art Carlson. He came to me and said that Graves was his snitch and anything I can do for him, he'd appreciate. He said the guy had made some big cases for him and he needed to keep him on the street. I figured what the hell, it was a chickenshit bust anyway. He was grateful. Promised to return the favor someday. I never got a chance to collect, though. I had to chase a fifteen-year-old over a fucking wall."

On the television, the woman had overbid on the merchandise and was looking forlorn. I, on the other hand, was trying to conceal my excitement. The case was finally coming together.

I stood up. "I want to thank you for your time, Mr. Hill."

He looked disappointed. "You gotta go so soon?"

"I'm afraid so."

"You don't mind if I don't get up," he said.

"Of course not," I said. "I hope you feel better soon."

"You'll probably be hearing from me when I do," he said.

"I'll be looking forward to it," I told him and left.

Thirty

Information had an Annette Hodges listed in Encino. The maid that answered the phone told me in broken English that Señora Hodges was not home but would be back around four. She did confirm that I had the right Señora Hodges, the one who had been married to a policeman. I drove out to Encino.

The house was a long, ranch-style house in a new, affluent development called Rancho Heights. I parked across the street and waited. At 4:14, a gray Acura Legend pulled into the driveway and a woman and a little girl got out. I stepped out of the car and trotted across the street.

"Mrs. Hodges?"

She turned. She was in her thirties; how far in, I couldn't tell. Her face was narrow, with nice bone structure, and she had dark, deep-set eyes. She wore very little makeup and needed very little. Her chestnut hair was pulled back and fastened. She had on an olive-green knit pullover blouse, a green plaid skirt, and knee-length boots.

The little girl was dressed in a blue uniform, the kind worn by Catholic school students. She was maybe ten, with a freckled face and dark brown pigtailed hair. Her arms were full of schoolbooks.

"Yes?" the woman asked.

I showed her my identification. "My name is Asch, Mrs. Hodges. I'm a private investigator."

"Like on TV?" the little girl asked.

"Almost," I said, smiling down at her. "What's your name?"

"Trisha."

"My name's Jake, Trisha. Looks like you've got a little homework there."

She made a face and nodded.

"What grade are you in?"

"Fifth."

Annette Hodges interrupted, "What's this about?"

"It's nothing for you to be concerned about, Mrs. Hodges," I said, and intentionally glanced down at her daughter to give her the impression that perhaps she should not be privy to our conversation. "Perhaps we could talk inside?"

She hesitated, then said, "Come in."

I followed them through the front door. The living room was spacious and plushly decorated with overstuffed chairs and a large sectional couch. There was a rattan bar along one wall and, behind that, sliding glass doors which looked out onto a wide patio. A squat, dark Aztec-looking maid dressed in jeans and a sweater came through a doorway and Annette Hodges said, "Hola, Christina. Anybody call?"

"Sí, señora. By the teléfono."

Annette Hodges said to her daughter, "Honey, you go with Christina and get something to eat."

"Yes, Mommy," the little girl said, then to me: "Nice to have met you."

"Nice to have met you, Trish."

She followed the maid into the kitchen and I said, "A beautiful little girl. And so well behaved."

"Thank you."

"She goes to Catholic school?"

She nodded. "St. Vincent's."

"That must be pretty expensive."

"It isn't cheap. But with public schools the way they are, there isn't much choice. Won't you sit down, Mr. Asch?"

"Thank you," I said, and sat on one end of the sectional.

She took a chair and crossed her legs. "Now what's this about?"

"Just a routine background check, Mrs. Hodges—"

She raised an eyebrow. "On me?"

I smiled. "No. On your late husband's partner. Leslie Boetticher."

She stiffened visibly.

"Is something the matter?"

"That's what I was going to ask you," she said. "Is Ms. Boetticher in some sort of trouble?"

"Not that I know of."

"Why are you doing a background check on her?"

"I'm afraid that's confidential."

She said coldly, "Well, I'm afraid if you're looking for some kind of recommendation about the woman's character, you won't get it here."

"Why is that, Mrs. Hodges?"

She clasped her hands in her lap. "She's the reason my daughter has no father."

I shook my head slightly. "I'm afraid I don't understand—"

"Fred was a loving husband and a good father before she became his partner. He cared about the job, sure, but his family always came first. Then she came along and he changed."

"Changed how?"

"He became distant. We hardly talked when he did come home. The silences became longer and louder. He used to love to play with Trish, but after a while he didn't even have time for that. Everything became the job, the job, the job. He spent all of his time on the streets trying to catch crooks. He tried to tell me he was doing it for us, but it wasn't for us. It was for him. And her. She seduced him."

Leslie did seem to have a problem with her partner's wives. I could see why. I wondered if Annette Hodges and I were seeing the same thing. "Are you saying they were having an affair?"

"If you mean a sexual relationship, I don't know. I wondered about it at times. I even asked Fred. He denied it. Actually, that might have been easier to deal with. When I said she seduced him, I meant it in another way. She seduced Fred with blind ambition."

"I'm not sure I understand—"

"She was obsessed with moving up in the department, making detective. That's all Fred started talking about. He started taking on overtime assignments, volunteering for night duty, going on off-duty surveillances. It got to the point he hardly came home at all. He spent all of his time on the streets, trying to make the big busts, rack up the stats. He said that was the key to all of our dreams, to being able to get the things we wanted. I tried to tell him all we wanted was him—alive." She stopped and stared at me. "She got what she wanted, at least. She made detective. By standing on the body of my husband."

"You're saying she got your husband killed on purpose?"

"Fred was a cop for four years before she came along. Talk to his first partner, Archie Blaisdell. Fred was never reckless. It was only after he got hooked up with her that he started to throw himself into dangerous situations. It was her. She talked him into it. She convinced him that the key to advancement was to impress the brass by making the big busts. They were always the first to roll on any call. The last one got him killed."

"The jewelry store."

She nodded. "He was awarded three citations for bravery beyond the call of duty. He was buried as a hero. That was all he got. No promotion, nothing but a hole in the ground. It made me sick to see her on TV every night, pretending to be so modest and self-effacing, talking with great sadness about her partner who so selflessly gave his life in the line of duty. She didn't care anything about Fred, except as someone to use to get a leg up. Ironic, but Fred was starting to share my opinion of her toward the end. Only, by that time, it was too late."

"What'd he say?"

"He'd begun to doubt her motives and his own. He admitted I was right about at least some of the things I said about her being only out for one person—herself. He began to finally question why he was jeopardizing everything—his family, his life—just for the privileges of wearing street clothes and making a few bucks. He promised me things were going to change." She sighed heavily. "They changed, all right. Permanently."

I got up. "Well, thank you for your time, Mrs. Hodges. I appreciate your talking to me."

She uncrossed her legs and stood. "I hope I've been some help to whoever you're working for. Ms. Boetticher deserves whatever she gets. God knows she took enough away from me."

Thirty-one

I called Hollywood Division. Leslie was out in the field, but Lyle Choquette was in. He told me she had just called to say that she was on her way in. I told him I'd be there in twenty minutes and to give her the message.

She still was not there when I arrived. Lyle came out of the back, looking rumpled as ever, and shunted me back to his desk. He cleared off the remnants of a chili burger wrapped in waxed paper and deposited it in his wastebasket, then sat down. He grinned lasciviously and shook his head in wonder. "You and the bitch goddess. Who would have thought?"

Grabner hadn't hesitated to spread the word. "She's a nice lady."

"She's more than that. Every guy around here has been dying to rip off a piece of that, but it's been the ice treatment. Someday, when you're not seeing her anymore, you're going to have to tell me what it was like."

I remembered something else about Lyle. He always drove with his hand out the window, squeezing the wind. Said it felt like a tit.

"How is she as a detective?" I asked, trying to get his mind off my sex life.

"Good," he said unequivocally. "I haven't got a lot of use for most women cops, but I gotta admit, she's got the instinct. She's smart, and once she gets her teeth into something, she never lets go. If I was a killer, I wouldn't want her on my tail, I can tell you."

"Were you around when she got shot in that jewelry store robbery?"

"Oh, yeah. She's lucky she's alive. Who would have thought that asshole would be carrying two guns?"

"You knew her partner? The one who got killed?"

"Hodges? Yeah. A hell of a nice guy. It was a real shame." He paused and tugged on his belt. "You know, after that went down and Leslie got promoted to detective, a lot of the guys bitched that it was only because she was a skirt, that if it'd been one of them, a shooting team would've been looking up their assholes, never mind getting bounced upstairs. But let me tell you, she pulled the department's fat out of the fire."

"How was that?"

"Remember that TV series that ran on corruption in the LAPD?"

How could I forget? "Yeah."

"Well, the department was taking flak from everywhere. Every yahoo liberal was after the chief's scalp, calling for him to be fired. Then the IAD started an investigation into those jewelry store robberies—"

"The string that Dotson pulled?"

"Right," Lyle said, nodding.

"Why would IAD be investigating that?"

"A couple of weeks before Dotson got blown up, a patrol car was rolling on a shooting call and saw a black-and-white parked in the alley behind the jewelry store right when the call came over the radio that the alarm at the store had been tripped. The two cops figured somebody had already rolled on the alarm and that the call they heard was a later call. The cops later said they probably were remembering things wrong because of all the shit that was coming down that night, but IAD started nosing around."

"Were they focusing their investigation on any cops in particular?"

He nodded. "They weren't saying, but word was they were looking very hard at the two patrolmen in whose patrol area most of the break-ins had occurred. McCaskill and I can't remember the other guy's name. Everybody was sweating it, especially the brass. All we needed right then was another scandal, and heads would start to roll. But then Leslie wasted Dotson and they found the crap he'd stolen from all the other robberies and the IAD investigation was called off. We needed a hero, bad, and we got one. Who gives a shit if it was a woman? Probably better it was. More PR. The women's libbers were happy, the mayor was happy, the chief was happy, the troops were happy. She saved everybody's ass, so I say screw these guys who bitch about her. They don't know her. She's a stand-up broad. I'd have her as my partner anytime."

"Carlson might have something to say about that."

He made a face. "That dickhead."

"You don't like Carlson?"

"I don't know too many people around here who do."

"Why is that?"

"He's just a miserable sonofabitch. He used to be an OK guy a few years ago, when I first got here, but he changed. Maybe it was his wife, I don't know, but he turned sour. Half the time, he comes to work gassed. It's gonna catch up with him one day soon. I don't know how Leslie puts up with his shit, to tell you the truth. She's gotta be a fucking saint." He looked past me and smiled. "Your ears burning, darling?"

Leslie walked over and sat on the edge of the desk. "You were talking about me?"

"In the most glowing terms," Lyle said.

She smiled at me and said, "I want to talk to you. Let's get out of here."

"Sure," I said, and looked around. "Where's Carlson?"

"Still off."

We said good-bye to Lyle, who had resumed grinning like a Cheshire cat, and went out into the reception area.

"Let's go get a drink," she said, her demeanor suddenly somber. "I need one."

"Something the matter?"

"Yes," she said. "I think there might be."

"Where?" I asked. "Code Three?"

She shook her head sharply. "No. No place where there are any cops. I'll drive. You can go with me."

She drove to a bar on Highland named Mickey's, a little hole in the wall just up from Santa Monica, one of those dark wood-paneled refuges for hangovers, kept icebox cool for the whiskey sweats, and dimly lit to soothe bloodshot eyes. The place smelled of stale beer, old leather, and cigarette smoke. The bar was full of daytime drinkers. We ordered a couple of beers from the bartender and took them over to one of the three empty booths in the back of the room.

She wasted no time starting. "After you left last night, Art came by. He was drunk. He made some lewd comments about you and me, and some derogatory comments about you."

I nodded. "He was waiting for me outside."

"What did he say?"

"None of it made much sense. He babbled some stuff about your ex-partner and warned me to stay away from you."

She looked at me strangely. "My ex-partner? Fred? What about Fred?"

I shrugged. "Like I said, none of it made much sense. Something about trains."

"Trains?"

"He said, 'She put me on the goddamn train, just like she put Hodges on, but I'm not getting off the same way.' Have any idea what he meant?"

She blinked, confused. "Absolutely none. What else did he have to say?"

"The only message that came through loud and clear was that he considered you his girl and I should stay away if I knew what's good for me."

She pursed her lips angrily and shook her head. "He came in and gave me about the same message. I hit the ceiling. I told him to stay out of my personal life, that I was emotionally as well as physically involved with you and that I intended to keep on seeing you as often as I could. He broke down and cried right in front of me, started blubbering that I couldn't do this to him, that I belonged to him, that he loved me and always had. It was embarrassing. I just stood there, stunned. I couldn't believe what I was hearing. I told him I liked him as a friend, but that was all and that was all I'd ever felt about him. I told him he should go check into Betty Ford or someplace and try to get his life in order. I also told him I was going to ask for another partner. That was when his wheels fell off completely. He started shouting that I couldn't do that to him, that everything he'd done, he'd done for us. I asked him what things, what was he talking about, and he said, 'Edith.'"

My pulse quickened. "What about Edith?"

Pain moved behind her face. "He said, 'I got rid of Edith so that we could be together.'"

"He told you he killed her?"

"I assumed that's what he meant, but I never asked him directly. To tell you the truth, I didn't want to know. I didn't want the responsibility. All I knew was that I wanted him out of my house and away from me. I felt like I needed time to think, especially after the question you'd asked earlier. I managed to get him calmed down and told him we'd talk about everything in the morning, and got him out of there."

"You did cover for him that day," I said.

She sighed heavily, nodded. "He told me he had a dental appointment at two o'clock, that it was the only time he could get in and he'd be back in an hour. He was gone for almost two. I called the dentist today. Art didn't have an appointment that day."

She withdrew into her own thoughts, shook her head. "I'm so damned confused, I don't know what to do, Jake. If he really did it, I can't keep it hushed up. But if it's just the liquor talking, I don't want to be the one to put him through the department wringer. It's hard for me to believe Art would do something as cold-blooded as that. I mean, I *know* the guy—"

"How well do you *really* know him?"

She looked at me curiously. "What do you mean?"

I watched her face closely. "Did you know that Graves was Carlson's snitch?"

The surprise in her eyes would have been difficult to fake. "What?"

"Carlson's kept him from going to the joint for a couple of years now."

"Who told you that?"

"A cop who pinched Graves a few years ago. Carlson came to him, asked him to go to bat for Graves."

Her brow furrowed. "Why the hell would Art keep that a secret? Why wouldn't he say anything about it when he found out Graves had been blown away?"

"The day Graves was killed, did Carlson do another one of his disappearing acts?"

"What day of the week was it?"

"Tuesday."

"He's off on Tuesdays. We both are." She shook her head, trying to absorb it all. "Wait a minute. Are you saying Art killed Graves?"

"You ever been on Carlson's boat?"

Again, her eyes registered surprise. "Boat? What boat?"

I was ninety-five percent sure she was telling me the truth. After all, she had volunteered the information about Carlson. So I told her about the paid-for cabin cruiser in the marina, the $130,000 Carlson had paid off on his house, and his new $30,000 car, which he had paid cash for. She listened, stunned, then shook her head. "I didn't know about any of this. The only car I've ever seen Art drive is an old beat-up van."

"I'm sure he only uses the Stealth for special occasions, like picking up payoffs from wealthy widows whose husbands have recently mysteriously disappeared."

I told her about Carlson's meetings with Shirley Melnick and Bellasario. She stared at me with her mouth open. "Are you saying Art is doing contract hits? I can't believe it."

"He's getting his money from somewhere," I said.

She shook her head, confused. "How does that fit in with Graves?"

I laid out the scenario. "What if Carlson's wife suspected he was into something crooked. She doesn't know who to go to on the police department, she doesn't know who else is crooked. She calls me, wants me to check it out. Carlson finds out somehow that she's made an appointment to see me and he wants to know what about. He has Lexine Woods cancel the appointment and has his snitch Graves send me out of town on a wild-goose chase tailing her, while Graves keeps the appointment in my office with Edith Carlson. She doesn't know what I look like, so she doesn't know she's not talking to me. She relays her suspicions about her hubby's criminal activities to Graves, hires him to get proof, and leaves. Carlson is listening in and knows he can't let Graves leave my office. He knows too much. He takes him out. So does his wife, so she has to go, too."

"And Lexine was part of it, so he did her, too."

"Right."

"What about Gilman?"

I shrugged. "Gilman and Graves were partners. Maybe he knew about the masquerade, maybe not. Doesn't matter if he did. He was the perfect fall guy. All Carlson had to do was plant the evidence in his room and shoot him up. Case closed."

"Jesus Christ," she said. "Have you told anybody else about any of this?"

"Not yet."

She put her hand on top of mine and stared into my eyes. "Do me a favor. Don't do anything until I look into it. Before I go to IAD with it I want to be absolutely sure. If he's dirty, if he's a killer like you say, I'll be the first to turn him in. But if you're wrong, and Art gets falsely crucified because of me, I'd never forgive myself. The man has been my partner for five years. I have to give him the benefit of the doubt as long as there is one. You can understand that, can't you?"

"Sure," I said, and paused. "Was Fred Hodges being investigated by the department at the time he was killed?"

Her eyes narrowed. "Why do you ask that?"

"I thought maybe that's the train Carlson was referring to."

"I doubt it. IAD was looking at Fred, but it was nothing, just bullshit."

"What was it about?"

"We arrested a guy, a black pimp named Rollins. He didn't like the way it was done, said that Fred roughed him up because he was black. Typical political bullshit."

I nodded, looked into her eyes. "What you told Carlson last night, about being emotionally involved, was that true?"

Her gaze dropped to the table. "From my end it is. I realize I can't speak for you. Why, does that surprise you?"

"No. I feel the same way." I stroked her hand. "It's just after the way things were left last night—"

She looked up searchingly. "That was why I felt hurt last night that you wouldn't trust me enough to level with me. I felt like we had something special going, and I thought you felt the same way. Maybe I was wrong." I was amused by the blush coloring her cheeks. The tough female cop could stare down the bore of a .38 without flinching, but was afraid to expose her emotions.

I tried to get a grip on my own emotions. I felt an electrifying exhilaration, and not just in my loins, which I constantly felt even thinking about her. I wanted more than that from her. I wanted to get close to her, to share everything, to inhale her, and the thought that she would feel even close to the same thing made me slightly giddy. "You weren't wrong."

I lifted her hand, kissed it gently.

She smiled and we stared at each other for a few moments. I was lost in her eyes. "That's why I had to tell you about Art. I didn't know who else to go to."

"We'll work it out," I tried to reassure her. "We'll work out everything."

She seemed preoccupied as she drove me back to my car. I got out and leaned through the window. "What are you going to do?"

"I'm not sure," she said, staring out the windshield. "Are you going home?"

"Yeah."

"I'll call you."

She tilted her head up and I leaned down and kissed her and she threw the car into gear and took off. I watched her squeal out of the lot, then walked to my car feeling oddly uneasy.

Thirty-two

A fog had started to roll in by the time I got home. I made myself a sandwich and lay down on the couch to watch the Lakers play the Denver Nuggets, but my mind wasn't on the game. I tried calling Leslie every half-hour but kept getting her machine. A knock on the door got me up.

Leslie stood on my front doorstep. She had on a long gray trenchcoat. It was soaked with blood. Her eyes were wide, wild. "I killed him," she croaked. "I had to."

She took a step toward me, her arms outstretched. Her hands were sticky with blood. I backed away in horror. "No. . . ."

The phone rang and I bolted upright. I was on the couch. I looked around, confused. The apartment was empty. On the television, some real estate scammer was saying how I could make millions by buying land for no money down. I looked at my watch. Twelve-twenty. The phone rang again.

"Yeah?"

"Jake?"

"Leslie?"

"Yes. You sound strange."

"You woke me up. I was in the middle of a bad dream."

"I know the feeling. I'm in the middle of one right now."

"Where are you?"

"At Art's boat. You were right. Art did the Melnick killing and probably a bunch of others. I have the proof."

"What is it?"

"I'll show it to you when you get here."

"Where's Carlson?"

"At home. How long will you be?"

"Twenty minutes."

"The slip number is 23. The boat's name is *Double Oh Seven*. I'll be on board."

James Bond's license to kill. Why not? That was how he'd financed the thing. I hung up and went into the bathroom. After splashing some cold water in my face, I slipped into a heavy sheepskin coat and sat down on the bed. From the nightstand drawer, I removed my Seecamp .25 automatic, made sure it had a loaded clip and one in the chamber, and dropped it in my coat pocket.

The fog was thick and chalky all the way down the coast. The marina parking lot was nearly empty when I pulled in and parked. The lights of Harpoon Harry's glowed invitingly through the fog; the tinklings of a piano inside sounded warm and friendly. I climbed over the gate and went down the pontoon.

Somewhere out in the fog, a buoy bell rang a lonely note. The black water made slapping sounds on the hulls of the sleeping boats as I walked down to slip 23. The cabin cruiser was smaller than most of the boats around it, but was still good-sized. I stopped at the boarding ramp and called out, "Leslie?"

No answer came back. She said she would be on board. I put my foot on the boarding ramp and hesitated. In my pocket, the Seecamp felt comforting in my grip. What was I worried about? Carlson was home. She'd checked. I stepped on board, went to the doorway leading down to the cabins. I bent down and called out, "Leslie?"

A noise behind me made me turn when my head exploded into light and I was falling forward. I hit the stairs with my shoulder and bounced down into the dark passageway, landing heavily on my back at the bottom. Dizzily, I struggled up onto all fours and found myself staring into the silenced muzzle of a large-caliber automatic.

"I told you to keep out of our business, Asch. You should have listened."

I brushed my pocket with my arm. The Seecamp was still there. My chance of getting it out before taking a couple of rounds was slim, but it was the only chance I had. I looked at the gun barrel. It didn't waver an inch. Wonderful. All day long, the man had the alcoholic shakes, but now his hands were cast in cement. His face was cast in cement, too.

I tried to stall. "Carlson, this is dumb. You can't get away with it—"

He grinned. "Sure I will. You'll just become part of the food chain. Food for the sharks."

"Just like Melnick."

"That's right. Just like Melnick. And half a dozen others."

"Including your wife."

"The stupid bitch. She overheard me talking to Shirley Melnick. She had to be smart. Like you. Only you ain't so smart."

My hand inched toward the coat pocket. "People know I'm here—"

He grinned and cut me off: "You mean my partner?"

I didn't like that grin. "Where is she?"

"She's around, don't worry."

"What have you done with her?"

"Done with her? You really *are* stupid."

Behind him, a long leg edged quietly down the stairway, then another. Leslie lowered herself into the cabin, her eyes fixed on Carlson's back. She raised her right arm and aimed the Beretta automatic at the middle of Carlson's spine. She took another step down and the wooden stair creaked loudly.

Carlson heard it, but it didn't seem to disturb him. He kept his eyes on me and said over his shoulder, "That you, Les?"

Her eyes were like shiny, hard marbles, her voice deadly serious. "Drop it, Art."

Confusion registered in his eyes and he started to turn around. I plunged my hand in my pocket just as three shots rang out in deafening, rapid-fire order and the front of Carlson's chest exploded in a shower of blood. He lurched and fell and I rolled to one side to keep it from being on me. He hit the floor with a thud, facedown, and was still. Leslie came down the stairs cautiously, her Beretta trained on Carlson's back where the three bullets had entered in a tight pattern. "You OK?" she asked, her voice tense.

I was hyperventilating. My voice was a croaking whisper. "I think so."

I stood up, and she kicked the gun from Carlson's outstretched hand. It clattered away in the corner and she bent down and felt his carotid for a pulse.

"Is he dead?"

She nodded and stood up, sighed and holstered her gun. Her pupils were widely dilated, giving her the appearance of an excited animal. "You got here sooner than I expected. I was in the bar next door. That's where I called you from. Thank God I checked the parking lot and saw your car. Ten seconds more and you would've been dead."

She threw her arms around me and held me close. While she clung to me, I asked, "Where did he come from? I thought you said he was home?"

"He was when I checked forty minutes ago. I never imagined he would come out to his boat in the middle of a foggy night."

"What was the proof you found?"

"Envelopes full of cash. And a diamond ring of Melnick's. He must have taken it after he killed him."

I looked down at Carlson. I wanted out of there as fast as possible. I wanted to be somewhere where there were lights and lots of people. "Let's get out of here. You can call this in while I get a drink."

"I can use one, too," she said.

There were only three other patrons at Harpoon Harry's bar. I sat at a table near the fireplace and ordered two doubles from the cocktail waitress. A few moments later, Leslie came in from the parking lot and sat down. "They'll be here in a few minutes. We should get back there as soon as we finish these."

"You can go back. I'm staying here."

"They'll want to talk to you—"

"They can come here and talk to me."

She gave me a concerned look. "Something the matter?"

"Where'd you find the money and Melnick's ring?"

"On the boat. There's a compartment below one of the bunks."

"Convenient."

She looked at me curiously over the rim of her glass. "What do you mean by that?"

"Keeping something incriminating from a job can be handy sometimes. You never know when you're going to need to use it. Presto, change-o, a little sleight of hand, and evidence materializes miraculously out of the air. Like Graves' wallet and the murder weapon being found in Gilman's room. Like stolen jewelry from those robberies years ago being connected to Dotson—"

Her eyes narrowed into slits. "Dotson? What does he have to do with anything?"

"That's where it started, didn't it? He was your partner on the heist jobs, wasn't he? Yours and Hodges's?"

"Have you flipped out?"

"Hodges had started to talk to his wife. Your hold on him was slipping. He'd become unreliable—like Carlson here—especially with the IAD nosing around. You saw a way to take care of both him and Dotson and squelch the IAD investigation at the same time. You set up the last burglary and brought a throwaway gun, which you shot your partner with after you shot Dotson with your service automatic. Only you hadn't counted on Dotson living after you'd put four into him, and you hadn't counted on him bringing his own gun along. That nearly screwed everything up for you permanently. But all's well that ends well."

She shook her head. "You can't really mean this. You can't think I killed my own partner—"

"How did you recruit him originally? Like you recruited Carlson? With sex? Like you recruited me?"

"You?"

"Sure. I'm your witness. I'm only alive because I'm living proof that you *had* to kill Carlson to prevent him from killing me."

"Tell me you're joking."

"I wish I were. Then maybe I wouldn't feel as stupid as Carlson said I was. You suckered me all the way."

"You know I love you," she protested weakly.

I smiled. "Carlson thought you loved him, too. That's how you got him to do what you wanted. That's how you got him to think I was coming here to get killed, when it was he that was being set up. He'd become a loose cannon, drinking too much, spending too much. He was obsessing on you, just like you counted on me doing. You used him to be the contact man, you pushed him up front to contract for the jobs and collect the payoff money. I wonder if Mrs. Melnick even knew you existed, that you were the brains running the show? Probably not, otherwise, you wouldn't be able to supply the proof that Carlson had done the dirty deed."

"You *are* crazy—"

"Carlson knew you were around. He said so before you shot him. But he was still going to kill me. He wouldn't have taken the chance if you hadn't been in on it."

Her silent stare cooled, turned icy.

"He heard you coming down the stairs of the boat, but he didn't even bother to turn around. But he called your name. He knew it was you. What he didn't know was that you were going to blow out his spine."

Her lips compressed tightly, but she still said nothing.

"He said something to me that should have tipped me. A little pronoun slip. He said 'I told you to keep out of our business.' Not 'my.' '*Our*.'"

She looked amused now. "Hardly proof of anything. Not even that Carlson was working with anybody, never mind with me."

"Proving isn't my business. That's for your colleagues to do."

Her demeanor changed suddenly. Her gaze thawed and she put her hand on top of mine and looked deeply, beseechingly, into my eyes. Her voice took on a slight quiver. "Jake, I'm begging you. We can have it all. You and me. I realize you're under a lot of stress. You nearly got killed tonight. That's what's making you say these crazy things. I realize that and I forgive you. But if you repeat these terrible accusations, it's going to tear us apart. I love you, you have to believe that."

She was good, I had to hand it to her. She almost had me convinced. When I looked at her, I saw an angel. A stone angel. I pulled my hand out from underneath hers. "Tell them I'll be right here."

Her face hardened again, like quick-setting cement. She stood up. "You're a fool."

"Funny, that's how I got into this case, trying to prove that I wasn't."

She looked down at me with a combination of pity and scorn. "The only thing you can prove is that I saved your life. You'll have to testify to that, unless you want to commit perjury. All the rest is merely conjecture on your part. Anyway, who do you think they'll believe? A broken-down bedroom spy or a decorated LAPD detective?"

"I guess we'll just have to wait and see."

I glanced past her where a couple of uniforms had just walked through the door. She turned and saw them, then glared at me and went to greet them. Even though she was across the room, her essence hung over the table like an unpleasant perfume, cloying and overpowering.

Thirty-three

The knocking on my apartment door interrupted my drinking. I got up and bobbed and weaved to the door. "Who is it?"

The voice said, "Guess."

I opened the door and Jan came in, smiling. "Did you see my story tonight?"

"'The Dark Side of the Force'? I saw it."

"What'd you think?"

"You should have done your standup in a Darth Vader outfit."

"Funny," she said, as if she didn't really think it was. I closed the door and she sniffed at my mouth. "You've been drinking."

"You have the nose of a true investigative reporter."

"Mind if I have one?"

"Help yourself," I said, flopping down on the couch and resuming my own drinking.

"The perfect host," she said, and went out to the kitchen, where the half-empty vodka bottle stood on the counter. She talked while she made herself a see-through. "Thanks for the scoop, by the way. The chief is going nuts. He wouldn't say much on camera, just that Internal Affairs is looking into the possibility that one or more Hollywood detectives were being investigated in connection with several homicides, but offscreen, he was pissed. Wanted to know where I got my information."

"Where did you get it? It didn't all come from me."

"I have a friend in IAD. He owed me a favor."

"It had to be a pretty big one."

"It was." She came out of the kitchen and sat down beside me. "I knew there was something wrong about her."

"Congratulations."

"Think they'll make it stick?"

I shrugged. "Depends if they find the money. Without that, there's really no proof. She was smart and careful. *Real* careful."

She smiled coyly. "She wasn't careful enough."

I looked at her hard. "What have you found out?"

"Tune in tomorrow."

I sat up. "I gave you the scoop, remember?"

"They've turned up two bank accounts, one in the Cayman Islands and one in Panama."

While I gave that some thought, she asked, "Have you heard from her?"

"No."

She came close and played with one of my shirt buttons. "Is that why you're drinking? Because of her?"

"Maybe."

"Poor baby," she said. "Let Mommy make it better."

I wasn't sure that she could, but I was willing to let her try.